GRANNY GOES HOLLYWOOD

A SECRET AGENT GRANNY MYSTERY BOOK 5

HARPER LIN

This is a work of fiction. Names, characters, organizations, places, events, and incidents are either products of the author's imagination or are used fictitiously.

GRANNY GOES HOLLYWOOD

Copyright © 2018 by Harper Lin.

All rights reserved.

ISBN: 978-1-987859-65-2

www.harperlin.com

ONE

Nothing much happens in Cheerville, at least on the surface. A sleepy bedroom district of a major city on the East Coast, it's all Colonial-style houses and manicured lawns. Topiary and book clubs are the main hobbies. Double-parking and late returns on library books are the major crimes. The last serious outbreak of public violence was a little skirmish during the Revolutionary War. After a bit of firing, both sides retreated. Cheerville is dull. Its people are dull, and that's how everyone wants it.

At least on the surface.

In fact, in my short time here since retiring from the CIA, I've uncovered murders, secret gambling rings, organized crime, and murder.

Yes, I said murder twice. There's a lot of murder here. Something about leafy, prosperous suburbs makes people want to kill each other. And yet these ruthless killings barely make a ripple on the placid life of this town. Most of the murders are never reported as such, and the content citizens of Cheerville go through their dull routines while I keep looking over my shoulder, wondering where the next danger will come from.

I'm Barbara Gold. Age: seventy. Height: five foot five. Eyes: blue. Hair: gray. Weight: none of your business. Specialties: undercover surveillance, small arms, chemical weapons, Middle Eastern and Latin American politics. Current status: retired widow and grandmother.

Addendum to current status: as excited as a teenybopper going to her first boy-band concert.

Why all the excitement in this excruciatingly non-exciting town? Because Cliff Armstrong is making a movie here.

If you are a woman, the name "Cliff Armstrong" is said with a catch of the breath followed by a long sigh. *Cliff! Aaaaarmstroooong.*

If you're a man, the name "Cliff Armstrong" is grunted in three short, powerful syllables like you're some maggoty new recruit addressing a psychotic Marine drill sergeant. *Cliff. Arm. Strong. Sir, yes, sir!*

Unless the guy is with his significant other, in which case he says nothing while giving annoyed sidelong looks at his girl as she swoons over the most rugged man in show business.

Cliff Armstrong is one of those rare action-movie actors who manages to appeal to everyone. His hairy-chested heroics are the role model for every man and adolescent boy in the country, while he always manages to show his softer side to appeal to the ladies.

In *Saving America III: The Final Showdown*, right in the middle of an epic fistfight with the Russian premier, Cliff Armstrong takes time out of kicking the vodka out of a spectacularly muscled evil politician to glance at the camera, wink, and save a kitten from being trampled by the Russkie. Then he proceeds to pound the greatest threat to American democracy into borscht.

In *Race Against Death*, he's chasing the bad guys when a truck suddenly blocks his way. He swerves to the side and crashes through the barrier of the overpass he's on, and his car goes flying over a sidewalk full of busy people. Cut to a little girl letting go of her balloon and crying as it floats away. Cliff Armstrong (you must always say his entire name, otherwise you spoil the effect) reaches out of the window and grabs the balloon as his car flies past. Once his car lands safely in a hotel swimming pool, splashing all the young women sunning themselves in their bikinis, he runs back to the little girl and gives her back her balloon.

It's that soft side to his character that gets the ladies truly swooning, not his chiseled features, square jaw, brilliant-blue eyes, perfect blond buzz cut, or impressive muscle mass.

Although all that helps, of course.

So, Cliff Armstrong was coming to our town to make a film called *Freedom's Hero: The Fight for America*, a historical action picture about the American Revolution. According to a breathless article in the *Cheerville Gazette*, the Hollywood folks had chosen our town because of its lovely town square. Actually, it's a triangle—because Cheerville rarely gets things entirely right—a giant triangle of manicured grass where our Colonial forefathers used to graze their cattle. To one side stands a church built in 1760 with a soaring spire. George Washington prayed there once. To either side of this church is a row of Colonial-style buildings, some of them actually from the Colonial period. On the other side of the town square (or triangle) is a little one-room schoolhouse from the early nineteenth century. On the third side is an eighteenth-century cemetery with the graves of several Revolutionary War soldiers as well as the early founders of the town. It's all very atmospheric and green and pleasant, and if you set the camera angles just right and use CGI to rub out the telephone poles, it looks like you're back in 1776.

Of course all this fuss upset the sleepy life of Cheerville. The entire town square had been cordoned off, and Police Chief Arnold Grimal had all his officers working overtime diverting traffic and controlling the crowds who came to the barriers to gape at all the film equipment and hope to catch a glimpse of everyone's favorite action hero.

I was among them, my aged heart going pitter-patter as I recognized the athletic figure of Cliff Armstrong step out of a trailer.

Oh, sorry. *Cliff! Aaaaarmstroooong.*

Sigh.

He was dressed as a Revolutionary War officer, complete with a tricorne, a blue jacket with bright brass buttons, and white tights that nearly caused half the crowd to faint.

The female half, that is.

To our surprise and delight, he waved at the cheering, swooning crowd and started to head our way. A man with a clipboard and headphones cut him off and said something, pointing at the grassy area where they were going to film a battle scene. A row of extras dressed as British soldiers faced a row of extras dressed as minutemen. Several cannons were set up, too, along with men on horseback who looked quite dashing until Cliff Armstrong came out of his trailer and eclipsed them.

The crewmember put a hand on the movie star's arm. Cliff jerked away with a snarl. A moment later, his face beamed at us as if nothing had happened and he walked right out of the movies and into our lives.

"He's actually coming over!" said Octavian, my new boyfriend.

Oh, had I not mentioned he was with me? I seemed to have forgotten all about him.

We stood behind a row of traffic barriers, with a couple of policemen and several security officers keeping us in check. I was amazed we didn't all break through the barrier, trample the cops and donut boys, and rush over to our hero.

But we stayed where we were. I think we all wanted to make a good impression.

If making a good impression meant shrieking and waving autograph books over our heads, that is.

"Hello, Cheervillians!" he said. "It's great to be here in your beautiful town on this beautiful day."

At least I think that's what he said. It was hard to hear over my shrieking, which reached an octave I hadn't been able to manage since age thirteen.

He went down the line, signing autographs,

shaking hands, and posing for selfies. When he came up to me and Octavian, he actually put his arms around both of us. I nearly had a coronary. Octavian looked close to cardiac arrest himself.

"It's so nice to see a happy couple still married after all these years," Cliff Armstrong said in his booming voice so all could hear.

Octavian and I gave each other an awkward glance. We had been dating for only a few months. Neither of us had the guts to correct our hero. In any case, he had already moved on. After more handshaking and selfies and autographs, including autographing one young woman's inner thigh, he stood back and raised his hands.

"Such a warm welcome. Thank you! Thank you! It's always nice to meet my fans." He put on an expression of mock worry. "You are my fans. Aren't you?"

"Yes!" we all screamed. Octavian looked like he was seventeen and not seventy. I suspect I looked the same. I certainly felt that way.

"Great!" Cliff Armstrong shouted. "Because we have a very special treat for you today. We're about to shoot one of the stunts for *Freedom's Hero: The Fight for America*. I'm the hero of course." He chuckled modestly. We roared with laughter.

"Now this is one of the battle scenes we're

filming today, and in it, I'm leading my men against the British. They outnumber us, as usual, but we don't care because we're Americans! There's going to be a lot of firing going on. Don't worry. All the muskets are loaded with blanks. You'll also see the cannons go off and explosions in parts of the town square, um, triangle. Keep back, and you'll be safe. Please cooperate with security so we can get a great shot.

"In the scene before this one, I'm in the church, professing my love to Liberty Smith. That's Gwendolyn Parker's character."

A grumble passed through the female half of the crowd. How dare that cheap two-bit actress get a series of love scenes with Cliff Armstrong.

"The British are going to move in from over there." He pointed to the opposite end of the village green. "And I'm going to rush out of the church and lead my men in a charge."

We applauded. He took off his tricorne and swept it down to his side as he gave us an old-fashioned bow. Then he continued. "So, we're going to do a few practice takes charging across the grass here. After that we'll go live with the special effects. That's when we'll be firing blanks and charges set in the grass will be going off. You'll see me fly in the air at one point. Don't worry, because that's not me.

It's my stunt double. And he won't really be getting hurt. A springboard hidden in the grass will make him fly forward, and a small charge between the springboard and camera will make it look like he's blowing up."

"You die in this movie?" some guy gasped.

Cliff Armstrong put his fists on his hips and let out a belly laugh. "Have no fear! You can't kill America! In the next take, I'll get up, brush myself off, and lead my men to victory!"

Everyone cheered. Cliff Armstrong flashed us a sparkling grin then turned and strode back to the set.

What followed started out surreal and ended up startling. The British soldiers moved to the far side of the village green, the men all in a row, with their muskets at the ready, flanked by their officers and some cavalry. A few cannons were set in front of them. I thought I recognized one of the mounted officers as a villain from another of Cliff Armstrong's movies, but I couldn't remember his name. The minutemen stood in a disorganized rabble in front of the church as if they weren't expecting an attack. Several cameras were set up in various locations—one close to the British line, one on a high crane for a bird's-eye view, another next to the front steps of the church, and two more at the midpoint of the village green, where I supposed the two sides would meet. They were all mounted on trolleys set onto what looked, for all the world, like miniature train tracks. This, Octavian explained to me, was so the cameras could move alongside the action to get smooth tracking shots.

The director, Vance Randolph, sat on top of a high chair that looked like what lifeguards use at the beach. He had a megaphone and a handheld radio. Sitting on either side of him were a couple of young and quite nubile female assistants.

"Okay, places, everybody," Randolph barked through the megaphone. "Ready? Okay, roll 'em!"

The British started marching across the green, the camera moving alongside them. The minutemen milled about in apparent fear, the camera near them focusing on one of the soldiers as he shouted, "Look!" and pointed at the approaching enemy.

Then the doors of the church burst open, and Cliff Armstrong rushed down the stairs, the camera by the steps moving alongside him. He shouted at his men to get in line, and they formed up.

The minutemen leveled their guns and fired.

Or at least pretended to. There was no sound, no smoke, but a couple of the British clutched their chests and fell. Then Cliff Armstrong drew his sword and shouted, "Charge!"

The minutemen charged. The British pretended to fire, and the minutemen started to drop. Then the British artillery officer shouted, "Fire!" and one by one the cannon crews went through the motions of shooting their pieces. Several minutemen threw themselves in the air and landed on the ground. Some were quite acrobatic about it. I supposed they were stuntmen.

"Cut!" Vance Randolph shouted through his megaphone. "Minutemen, you're coming up too fast. We want to draw this battle scene out. British Soldier Number Forty-Three, you're supposed to fall on the first volley. Why are you still standing?"

"Sorry! I'll get it right next time," British Soldier Number Forty-Three called back in a nasal Bronx accent.

"How inconsiderate of him not to die on cue." Octavian chuckled.

The scene was set up again. The British entered the village green. Cliff Armstrong rushed out of the church, and the battle ran through its paces once more. This time one of the minutemen fell on the first volley instead of the second like he was supposed to, and Cliff Armstrong didn't shout "charge" loud enough, so it was back to the starting line.

"If only all wars could be fought this way," Octavian said, "it would save a lot of hardship and suffering."

This went on for a couple of hours. Some spectators drifted away, only to be replaced by newcomers. Octavian and I stayed, because we both admired Cliff Armstrong (for very different reasons) and because we were curious to see the stunts and special effects when they were finally played for real.

We got more than we bargained for.

The director blared into his megaphone again. "Okay, folks. Let's get down to it. Stuntmen, take your places. This is the last rehearsal before we set off the explosives. Soldiers and artillery people, load your weapons with blanks. We want the effect of the smoke for cameras one, two, and three, but we're going to hold off on the ground explosions until the final take."

The actors and extras loaded their muskets. While I've never gone for black-powder shooting like some hobbyists and hunters, preferring modern efficiency over nostalgia, I'd always appreciated antique weapons demonstrations.

Of course these were modern replicas, but they loaded the same way. The soldier took a premeasured charge of powder wrapped in a paper cylinder, tore off the end of it with his teeth, and poured the powder down the barrel. In real life the packet would also contain a bullet, but of course these didn't. Then the paper would be rammed down the barrel with a ramrod to make a seal before the bullet was put in. A small amount of black powder was also put in the firing pan. Then the lock was pulled back. This had a wedge of flint that, when the trigger was pulled, would snap down, striking a steel plate and sending sparks into the pan. The powder in the pan would ignite, and a small hole leading from the pan to the gun barrel allowed the powder inside to ignite. *Boom.* Bullet goes flying out. The artillery worked pretty much the same, except with a slow-burning match to light the powder in the pan instead of flint and steel. A beautiful bit of old-school engineering and physics.

Well, beautiful if you aren't on the receiving end.

Once everyone had loaded their weapons, the director told the cameras to roll, and the whole scene played out again. Cliff Armstrong rushed out of the church and got his men lined up. The British fired, flame and smoke blasting from their muskets, and a few of our boys fell. The minutemen fired back, and some of the redcoats fell.

"Looks like everyone's finally dying at the right time," Octavian said.

"They're professionals," I replied with a giggle. I'd taken to giggling around Octavian sometimes. I'd never been much of a giggler. He could have that effect on me, though.

"Charge!" Cliff Armstrong shouted.

The minutemen charged. The redcoats hurriedly reloaded and fired. More of the American patriots fell.

The cannons opened up with a boom, and I was surprised when an explosion burst right in front of Cliff Armstrong. I thought they were holding off on those until the final take.

Cliff Armstrong apparently thought the same. He stumbled back, mouth agape.

Another explosion burst to his right. All the extras froze in shock. The director shouted something in the megaphone that I didn't catch. Cliff Armstrong ran to the left in an obvious panic …

… and straight into the next explosion.

His body flew several feet in the air and came down with a thud.

As soon as it hit the churned-up earth, I knew he was dead. The body landed with a flop, completely limp, arms and legs askew. Living bodies do not do that. Trust me. I know.

For a second there was no sound except for the ringing in our ears.

"Medic!" Vance Randolph shouted through his megaphone. "We need a medic on the set!"

Then people started screaming. Some of the extras ran to Cliff Armstrong, clustering around his body and hiding him from view. A man carrying a medical case with a big red cross on the side rushed from behind one of the cameras, pushing aside the extras.

Then something happened that made everyone turn.

Cliff Armstrong ran out from the church.

TWO

"What happened?" we could hear him shout from above the hubbub.

"He's alive!" a woman shouted.

The medic had cleared away the extras, and we could see him kneeling by the torn body of Cliff Armstrong, while another Cliff Armstrong stared from the edge of the village green.

"Bert!" the living Cliff Armstrong said. "It's Bert, my stunt double." He turned to the crowd of fans. "I'm all right, everyone. It was only my stunt double!"

The fans cheered, which I thought was rather inconsiderate to poor old Bert.

Cliff Armstrong took another look at the torn-up village green with its three craters smoking from the recent explosions, and a shudder ran through his body. His rugged features disintegrated into a wild, panicked expression, and he ran off into the warren of trailers and trucks the film crew had set up on a side street. Within a moment he was gone.

And we were gone a moment later.

"Everyone needs to leave now!" a security man shouted. He looked like he was in charge. "Guys, get these people out of here!"

The cops and security people moved in. The security guard nearest to us said, "Filming is over for the day, folks. You need to go on home." As he said this, he ducked under the barricade, stretched out his beefy arms, and began walking toward us, a very effective way to make us move back. The other security guards, joined by the police, did the same.

"What happened?" someone asked.

"An accident," the security man replied. "A terrible accident."

Was it? I glanced in the direction of Vance Randolph. The director looked livid, shouting and waving his arms at a group of people standing at the foot of his high chair. One of them had raised his hands in a confused gesture, obviously protesting innocence.

The explosions hadn't been planned until the next take. I could understand one going off by accident, although with a professional Hollywood crew, even that was unlikely, but three explosions? Someone had been trying to kill Bert.

But why? And why in such a public fashion?

We walked a couple blocks to where Octavian had parked. Neither of us said a word. Octavian had been stunned into silence. My mind, on the other hand, was going a hundred miles an hour.

"Could you take me home?" I asked. "After that, I think I need to rest."

More like think through this murder and do some background research.

Back home, with my tortoiseshell kitten, Dandelion, curled up in my lap and a hot cup of tea by my side, I scoured the Internet for information about Cliff Armstrong, Vance Randolph, and anyone else I could find associated with the production of *Freedom's Hero: The Fight for America*.

I ended up with more information than I could handle. Any movie with stars this big attracts a huge amount of attention. There were entire websites and discussion groups devoted to the film, and they had barely begun filming.

Narrowing it down, I searched for a stuntman named Bert associated with the picture. Bert Raffers, twenty-eight, and a dead ringer for Cliff Armstrong. No wonder they hired him. It turned out he had been the star's stunt double in several pictures. I couldn't find out much more about him, though. He had virtually no online presence except a Facebook page switched to private. I saw no reason why anyone would have wanted to kill him.

Could they have intended to kill Cliff Armstrong? That didn't make sense, though, because whoever killed him had access to the explosive charges and was thus associated with the film. The director had called for the stuntmen to get into place, so the killer would have known it was Bert running across that field. Even if they had intended to kill the nation's biggest action star, I didn't see any motive.

I didn't see any motive for either of them.

I leaned back in my chair and sighed, stroking Dandelion as she purred contentedly on my lap. Staring at the screen for the next several minutes didn't give me any new ideas. For the moment, this case had me stumped. I simply didn't know enough to make any inroads into this mystery.

Unfortunately, that meant my next step would be going to see someone who almost always knew less than I did.

I was merciful on Police Chief Arnold Grimal. I didn't visit him until late in the afternoon. No doubt the poor man was swamped with enquiries from the film director and crew plus frantic calls from big-shot producers in Hollywood, all while trying to lay down the groundwork for a murder investigation.

A groundwork made of sand. Grimal was useless at anything more than directing traffic and handing out speeding tickets.

When I showed up at the police station, it was abuzz with activity. I passed Vance Randolph heading out the door, fuming with obvious stress and flanked by two men in expensive business suits who looked like lawyers. Through the glass partition that screened off the front end of the station from the offices in back, I saw a very stressed Arnold Grimal spot me, roll his eyes, and flee into his office.

After fast-talking the desk sergeant, who had become accustomed to my unannounced visits to his boss, I went to the back and knocked on the police chief's door.

"Busy," Grimal grumbled from the other side. I opened the door.

To my astonishment, Grimal really did look busy, a rare state of being for him. He had a phone to his ear and was typing furiously on his computer. Even stranger, there weren't any boxes of Chinese takeaway on his table.

Grimal put his hand over the phone and told me in a harsh whisper, "I said I was busy."

"I'll wait," I said, closing the door behind me

and sitting down without being invited. I was never invited. I had to invite myself.

Grimal went back to his phone.

"Yes, sir. A most terrible tragedy, sir. Yes, we have every man on it. Yes, I'm calling in overtime on all my officers. Yes, we'll find the suspect."

After a few more minutes of cringing yeses, Grimal finally got off the phone, leaned so far back in his chair I thought he'd topple over, and let out a big sigh.

"State police?" I asked.

"No," he said, rubbing his eyes. "Some important producer in Hollywood. They're all flipping out over there. They're convinced the explosion was meant to kill Cliff Armstrong and not Bert Raffers."

"What do you think?"

"It was murder," he said with a moan. "Oh, God, why does this have to happen on my watch?"

Grimal was being uncharacteristically astute.

"Why do you think it was murder?"

"These guys are pros. As far as I can see, no accident like this has ever happened on a major Hollywood movie set. Plus, Cliff Armstrong was supposed to be running across that field, not Bert."

"But the director called for all stuntmen to be on the set."

Grimal nodded. "I know, but Cliff Armstrong is like a lot of the big action stars. He likes to do his own stunts or get as close to them as the insurance people allow. If the studio had its way, he wouldn't come near any of those explosives, even when the safety is switched on like it was supposed to be."

"So, who was at the switch and set off the explosives?"

"Not the head stunt technician. He was away from the switchboard, talking with one of his assistants. We have several witnesses to that."

"So, someone could have walked over to the switchboard and blown up anyone on that field? That's pretty poor security."

Grimal shook his head. "The switchboard is encased in a heavy-duty steel box that can be shut and locked any time the technician walks away for even a minute. Then the electrical connection is disconnected. As soon as the explosions happened, the head technician and several other people rushed over to see what was going on. The box was still locked and disconnected."

"Huh," I said. Not a very intelligent thing to say, but I had nothing better.

"Huh," Grimal agreed.

"So why did the stuntman run out into the field instead of Cliff Armstrong?"

"Not sure. I've brought over a couple of plain-clothes police officers from Apple Bluff. I can't use any of my guys because they've been all over the set for the past few days. They'd be recognized. The Apple Bluff guys will check things out."

"Wait. They're going to continue filming?"

"Yeah. There are hundreds of millions of bucks hanging on this. The producer explained that if they shut down for even a few days, they'd lose millions and the production schedule might have to be pushed back. That means it wouldn't get out in time to be next summer's blockbuster."

I raised my hands in frustration. "A man's been killed!"

Grimal sighed and rubbed his temples. "I know, I know. I tried to talk them out of it, but they wouldn't listen. When I threatened to shut them down anyway, I got a call from the governor telling me to mind my own business. That's how he put it. 'Mind my own business.' Like this isn't my business!"

This last statement came out as an infantile whine. As much as I looked down on Grimal, I had to sympathize with him on this one. These Holly-wood people were being greedy and stupid. If the murderer would go to such lengths to kill someone this famous this publicly, he or she would be sure to strike again.

"Why is the governor coming down on you?"

"He and Vance Randolph went to college together. They're old drinking buddies."

"Wonderful."

Grimal stood. "Anyway, I have a lot of work to do. I appreciate you coming to check this out but—"

"I'll get to work."

Grimal's face turned into a mask of existential despair.

"B-but ..."

"Don't worry. I'll be discreet. Besides, if I crack the case, you know I'll hand over the credit to you, just like with that secret casino."

Grimal's eyes strayed to the plaque on the wall, an award given to him by the governor for excellent police work busting a hidden gambling ring in Cheerville. Actually, he had been covering it up to help out an indebted relative until I changed all that. To be fair, he did help out in the ensuing gunfight, but I did the vast majority of the work.

But I have to hide my past in the CIA, so I never get to take credit for anything. One of the downsides of the job, and it doesn't stop being a downside after you have supposedly retired.

Grimal's face lit up with sudden inspiration. Inspiration was so rare with that fellow that I did a double take. "You can't go onto the set," he said, pointing at me. "Only cast and crew are allowed on, plus the police."

For a moment I was stumped. Grimal beamed at me like a happy cartoon lighthouse. The beam switched off pretty quick once I remembered something I had read in the *Cheerville Gazette*.

"They're looking for extras. I'll sign on as an extra. That's how your plainclothesmen are getting on the set. Isn't it?"

Grimal groaned. His eyes rolled back in his head, and he fell onto his chair.

I waited for him to say something, but he looked temporarily paralyzed. I reached over his desk, patted him on the shoulder, and left.

It looked like I was going to be in the movies.

THREE

Joining a major Hollywood production proved easier than I thought and far less glamorous. I checked the ad I had seen in the *Cheerville Gazette*. It gave a local address and office hours and noted that they were looking for people of all ages and both sexes. "Costumes provided." That sounded nice. While my grandson complained that my clothes were too old-fashioned, nothing in my wardrobe could pass for eighteenth-century fashion.

The address was in a small office building a little away from the town center. The production company had taken over an entire floor and most of the parking lot. As the elevator doors opened, I was confronted by a burly security guard.

"Can I help you, ma'am?" he asked in that tone that security guys always use, which manages to be both polite and menacing at the same time. It sounded a little extra menacing since he turned up the volume. People do that a lot with senior citizens. He did not move out of my way, leaving me standing in the elevator.

I put on my sweet little old lady smile. "I'm here to apply for the job of extra for the movie."

"Oh, right." Mr. Menace stepped aside. "Second door on the left. You want the assistant casting manager."

"Oh, thank you, young man. So exciting to be in the movies, isn't it?"

"I wouldn't know, ma'am."

The door he indicated was open. Inside was a small office with little more than a digital camera on a tripod facing a white backdrop, a desk, and a frazzled woman in her thirties sitting behind it. She was typing like mad on a laptop. I knocked lightly on the doorframe.

"Oh, thank God!" she shouted as she saw me.

"Um, is everything all right?"

She sprang up from behind the desk. "Please tell me you're here to be an extra."

She was almost shouting, but I don't think it was because I was on the wrong side of seventy. I got the impression that she always shouted. Five takeaway cups of coffee and half a dozen soda cans sat on her desk. I suspected they were all empty.

"I am. Are you the assistant casting manager? Do you have an opening?"

"Do I have an opening? I have a giant, huge gap! I have a Grand Canyon of unfilled positions. Getting extras in this hick town is almost impossible. Do you have any acting experience?"

As a secret agent, I had been acting for most of my professional career.

"I've done some theater," I said, which was true in a way. "I've never been in a movie."

Unless you include a training video on how to throw grenades.

"It doesn't matter!" the woman said, waving her arms in the air. "You're the right age. We need old people."

"Well, I'm glad someone does."

"Here, let me get some head shots." The assistant casting manager hustled me to a spot between the backdrop and the camera. I was surprised. No one hustled people my age. It was more than a bit rude, but I'd deal with some hustling as long as I could get onto the set.

She busied herself with the camera, hands twitching, feet shuffling. It seemed this woman found it impossible to stay still.

"There are decaffeinated brands, you know," I offered.

"Waste of money. Smile, please. Now look frightened. Angry. Patriotic."

"What does looking patriotic look like?"

"Pretend you're seeing the American flag for the first time."

"Is Betsy Ross in this movie?"

She looked at me over the camera. "Who?"

"Betsy Ross."

"Is she some local actress? Is she available?"

"No, she designed the first American flag."

"Wow! Do you have her phone number? I'll call her right away."

"I don't think she's alive."

"Oh, well." She shrugged, bending behind the camera again. I tried to look patriotic, imagining myself at the opening of one of my grandson's soccer games, when the star of the high school chorus would come out to sing the Star-Spangled Banner. A nice gal, but her singing voice was so bad her rendition of the national anthem verged on treason.

"I said look patriotic, not bored and slightly horrified," the woman grumbled. "Never mind. You'll do."

"What are these photos for? I'm just going to be

in the crowd scenes, right?"

"Mr. Randolph likes to inspect each extra we hire."

"Especially the female ones?"

The assistant casting manager laughed. "Don't worry, honey. I'm thirty-five, and *I'm* too old."

"Likes spring chickens, eh? How original in a Hollywood director." Sarcasm isn't really my forte, but this time it came out naturally.

She gave a little shrug. "Oh, he's not so bad. It's all consensual, and they're all of legal age. Do you know he's memorized the age of consent in every state in the union and most foreign nations?"

"The second part of your statement doesn't support the first."

"You sound like my high school English teacher."

"Do I have the job?"

"Of course you have the job!" she replied, thereby confirming that it was her decision and not the director's, meaning he really did want to check out the photos for potential conquests and not for any professional reason. I was curious about this aspect of his character. It sounded like the sort of thing that could cause disruption and rivalry among a group of egotistical people stuck together on a high-stress project. I'd seen the same dynamic on missions.

"Is Mr. Randolph very forward?"

The assistant casting manager chuckled. "You've obviously never been to Hollywood. He's not nearly as bad as some people in this business. Stardom and wealth act like magnets to some women, especially if they are aspiring actresses. It's not so much that we're getting groped on the set. It's that women fling themselves at the stars and then get tossed away like an empty pizza box the next morning."

"Oh dear. Who should I watch out for? I mean, I know some young gals among the extras. Who should they watch out for?"

"Like I said, there's not much harassment on this set," she replied as she handed me a form and a pen. "Please fill this out. The problem is when the girls go for one of the guys, thinking they'll be the special one and won't get rejected like all the rest. They always do. Some are dumb enough to go off with one of the other actors, and the whole thing repeats itself. The bigger the star, the worse they are."

"Like Vance Randolph."

"And Cliff Armstrong. He's the worst because he's the sexiest."

Bingo. I had a hunch it would be something like this. I was never one to believe in stereotypes, but sometimes stereotypes exist because they are at least partially true. Casting couches and passing around young starlets like a game of fleshy musical chairs had been a part of the Hollywood scene since the silent era.

That thrill I always get when I find a piece of the puzzle was dampened by the discovery that my screen idol had feet of clay. A girlish reaction, I know, but I couldn't shake it. Cliff Armstrong had such a way with the crowds, like when he picked Octavian and me out of the group and mistook us for an old married couple. His work with charities was unrivaled. He gave millions away to worthy causes and pulled stunts like showing up at people's houses who had sent him fan mail and hanging out for the afternoon. He wouldn't even bring cameras along when he did these things. It wasn't for the publicity; he did it just to give back to his fans.

I had really admired him and believed that he was different from the usual plastic people Hollywood created. If what this frazzled assistant casting manager said was true—and she should know—he was no different from the rest of them.

My disappointment must have been apparent

on my face because the woman who had just hired me put a hand on my shoulder.

"Don't worry about it. You have to have tough skin in this business, even if you're a nameless extra. Look, you get a hundred bucks a day, free food, and get to see yourself on the big screen. So what if you see some skeezy stuff going on? There are worse jobs."

Like hunting down Salvadoran drug lords? Yeah, there were worse jobs.

I started to fill out the form and heard the assistant casting manager breathe a sigh of relief. She really must have been short on old people. I would have suggested Octavian or some of the folks from my reading group if there hadn't been a murderer loose on the set. Better to keep them away.

The form stipulated that I gave up all rights to royalties or how my image could be used. There was also a waiver stating that in case of injury, sickness, or death, neither the production company nor any of its employees could be held liable. I may have shivered a little as I signed that section.

"Great!" She snatched the form out of my hands as if I might change my mind at the last moment and handed me an ID card. "This card will get you on the set. First you need to go to costuming. They're those two big trailers you saw in the parking lot."

WHEN I GOT to the trailers, I was guided to the right one by someone singing George Michael's "Freedom" at the top of his lungs. I peeked in through the half-open door and saw the interior jam-packed with racks of Colonial-era clothing, everything from ragged slave shirts to fine dresses to British uniforms.

The song continued in a high falsetto.

"Hello?" I called.

The song cut short and a tall, quite-handsome man in his forties poked his head around a pile of leather boots. His best feature was the luxuriant black curls that fell to his shoulders. His worst feature was his fashion sense. He wore a Hawaiian T-shirt, pink shorts, and flip flops. He looked like he should be knocking back Piña Coladas in Boca Raton, not helping run a major motion picture.

"Are you here for costuming?" he asked in a singsong voice.

"Yes." I produced my card.

"Fabulous! We desperately need an old crone."

"I'm hardly at the old-crone stage."

He put a hand on my shoulder like that frazzled woman had. These Hollywood people were a touchy-feely bunch.

"Oh, honey, you must be new. I didn't mean to say you're a crone. No, you're very well-preserved. But we can apply a bit of makeup and age you twenty years."

"That's not the effect makeup usually advertises."

The costume director wasn't listening. He was too busy rummaging through the racks of costumes and holding one costume after another up to me. All looked very grungy and tattered. Perfect fashion for an old crone, I suppose.

After several tries, he threw his hands in the air.

"I give up! It just won't work! You don't fit."

I blinked. "Does that mean I can't be in the movie?"

He shook his head. "I'm afraid not. We need a crone, and you are simply too sweet looking."

For a moment, I couldn't think of a response. I felt stumped. I'd never been complimented out of a case before.

FOUR

"I'm sure I could play the part if you just gave me a chance," I pleaded. I needed this role. How else could I investigate the murder? If I left it to Grimal, the killer would get away. Even worse, Cliff Armstrong might get killed the next time instead of a stunt double.

"No," the costume director said with a sigh, hanging up the tattered rags.

"What about some crowd scenes? Couldn't I be some sweet little old lady watching the battle?"

The costume director threw up his hands. "No one wants to see sweet little old ladies watching battles! It doesn't make any sense! Even if it did make sense, it would be as dull as dirt. When Vance Randolph shoots a crowd scene, he doesn't want just the same old, same old. He wants vivacity! Vitality! Verve! Vivaciousness!"

"And vacuousness too, no doubt."

He pointed at me like some demon from the lower depths of hell about to lay down a curse and said in a solemn voice, "No, that is exactly what he doesn't want. Every member of a crowd scene must have their own distinct characteristics. Old people just fade into the woodwork. It's like they're not there at all."

I put my hands on my hips and glared at him. "Young man, we are not invisible. One day you'll be old, too, assuming someone doesn't run you over with a Mack truck for being so disrespectful. Disrespecting the elderly is disrespecting your own future!"

The costume director stared at me, mouth agape. For a second, I thought he was going to sputter out an apology. Instead he burst into laughter.

I stood there, fuming. Before I got a chance to give him a few choice words, he grabbed me by the shoulders again.

"If you were a man, I would kiss you. Instead let me give you a hug." He hugged me before I could say yes or no. "I can't believe I didn't see it before. You are perfect for the role!"

Despite his change of mood, I frowned at him. "What, I give you a little lecture, and now I'm perfect for the crone role?"

He looked confused for a moment then threw his arms wide. "The crone? No! I want to give you a speaking role! Old Widow Margaret Goode. She helps Cliff Armstrong defeat the British. No one suspects her because she's old, you see? A British officer is staying at her house and making her wait on him hand and foot, and when his fellow officers come over, he talks about their plans for a secret attack on the American camp. Old Widow Margaret Goode listens to it all and tells Cliff Armstrong, who then saves the day."

For a moment, I was stunned into silence. Me, in a speaking role next to my film hero? Unbelievable.

I'd like to say that I jumped at the chance since it would get me that much closer to him and help me with the case, but no such thought even crossed my mind. My mind was too full of adolescent fantasies of him falling in love with his supporting actress and sweeping me off my feet.

Reality intervened soon enough, thankfully. It's the old CIA training. Nothing like having to fight terrorists and international drug dealers to make you cynical.

"Wouldn't Mr. Randolph have to decide that?" I asked.

The costume director tut-tutted. "Of course, but he's a rubber stamp in this case. He only concerns himself with the important roles."

Or the young ones, I added silently.

"I would have thought you already had that part filled."

"We did, but the actress had a heart attack a couple weeks ago. Occupational hazard when you work with old people. We've been trying to find someone to fill the slot, but we haven't had any luck, at least not until today. Now, I suppose you don't have any acting experience, otherwise you would have come in here bragging about how you deserve something better than being an extra, but don't worry. We have dialog coaches and acting coaches and all that. We'll get you through. It's only a few lines anyway."

"I … um …"

The costume director gave me a hopeful look. "Please say yes. It pays well."

"Of course I'll do it," I managed to choke out at last. I was already getting jitters about having to work next to Cliff Armstrong.

"Brilliant," he squealed, clapping his hands. "I'll set it all up."

He pulled out a cell phone and had a long conversation with some secretary, who shifted him to a higher secretary, and then to the casting director. This got him referred back to the frazzled assistant casting director I had seen, because the casting director was having plastic surgery down in Mexico. I gathered all of this from the side of the conversation I could hear. What confused me was why the costume director didn't seem surprised that a person in such an important position would be going under the knife in a foreign country when there were vacancies in what was intended to be next summer's blockbuster.

When he finally got off the phone, I asked about that.

The costume director tittered. "Well, of course he can go to Mexico! He's getting a chin implant and a tummy tuck. You have to understand priorities in this business. Lovers are more important than family, the film is more important than lovers, and plastic surgery is more important than anything."

"I see," I said. I didn't.

"Anyway, honey, you're hired. I told Quinten we had a brilliant new talent for the role of Margaret Goode and that you didn't have any chronic health issues that might kill you off before we finish your scenes." He gave me an appraising look. "You don't, do you?"

"Not that I know of."

"Brilliant! You're hired. I'll send you over to the acting coach right away and get you up to speed."

THE ACTING COACH was a man named Harvey Miller, and Harvey Miller was passed out drunk when I met him.

He had an office in one of the little trailers that filled up what used to be one of the main roads through Cheerville, now blocked off to serve as a sort of annex to the filming going on in the town square. A good quarter mile of a two-lane road, plus many of the adjoining driveways and parking lots, had been taken over by a small town of trailers. Signs showed which offices or dressing rooms each were, and there was even a map on a poster board at the entrance. The security guard studied my ID badge for a moment and let me in. There was no picture on my badge, so it didn't count as identification. Their security wasn't all that tight, it seemed.

Nor was their professionalism. As I said, Harvey Miller was blotto when I got to his trailer.

The door was open, and after knocking repeatedly on the doorframe and not getting a response, I peeked inside.

A short, paunchy, balding man lay facedown on the floor, still gripping an empty bottle of whiskey as he snored gently. The room stank of alcohol.

Besides the half-dead body of my supposed acting coach, the trailer had a fridge, a kitchenette, a couple of chairs, and a desk with a computer and stacks of papers bound in those little black plastic circle thingies that always catch on your clothing or come unwound after reading through the pages more than once.

I stared at Harvey Miller for a moment, nonplussed, then went over to the next trailer, which identified its occupant as "Bill Nestor— Acting Coach."

Bill Nestor was vertical and quite annoyed that I interrupted him coaching a cute little blond boy of about eleven. They sat on chairs, facing each other, each holding a script in his hands and both looking like they were in a bad mood.

"I'm in the middle of important work," Bill informed me.

"My acting coach is passed out drunk."

"Harvey, right?" Bill groaned.

"Of course it's Harvey, dumbass," the boy said. "He's the biggest lush in the business."

"Is that any way to talk about your elders?" I asked the child.

"Shut up. I make more money than you do," the boy snapped.

I was so taken aback that I was struck speechless. Bill got up.

"Wait here, Evan. I'll be right back."

He walked out of the trailer, and I followed.

"Charming young man you have there," I commented.

"He's a little piece of trash I'd love to stuff in a dumpster," Bill grumbled. "But he's a rising child star, and Vance Randolph thinks he'll help sell the movie."

Then I realized I'd seen the child on a television sitcom a year or two before.

"He's a bit young to have fame go to his head," I said.

"Ha! You must be new," Bill said as he entered Harvey's trailer, stepped over his body, and went to his desk.

"People keep saying that to me."

Bill rummaged through the stack of bound papers.

"What's your role again?"

"Margaret Goode."

"Let's see. Margaret Goode. Margaret Goode. Oh, here we go."

He handed me a thick script.

"This is the script for the entire movie. Best to familiarize yourself with the whole thing. You have three scenes. They're marked with the red tags. They're shooting those scenes the day after tomorrow, so memorize those lines quick."

"The day after tomorrow?" I yelped. "How am I supposed to get ready?"

Bill grinned and gave Harvey's body a kick.

"I suggest you start by waking up your acting coach."

"Can't you coach me?" I pleaded.

"Me? No, I have to spend all my time with that half-pint monster who just insulted you."

"Bill, hurry the hell up!" the monster in question shrieked from the other trailer. "We got work to do, you unprofessional loser!"

Bill rolled his eyes, grabbed a contract off Harvey's desk, and handed it to me. "You can't take the script until you sign a nondisclosure agreement."

"My hand is cramping from all the forms I keep signing," I complained.

Bill looked at me. "My hand is cramping from resisting the urge to spank that little brat in my trailer."

"Bill, get your ass in here!" the kid bawled.

"Why don't you stop resisting that urge?" I asked.

"And get fired, sued, and brought up on charges? No, I'll take the daily stress and humiliation. Thank you very much."

I signed the contract. Bill forged Harvey's signature, and he left with a sigh. A moment later, I could hear him enduring a torrent of abuse. I closed the door to spare my ears.

That didn't spare my nose. With the air circulation cut off, the stench of alcohol became almost overpowering. I gritted my teeth and endured it.

Since I was alone, my first instinct was to do some snooping. I didn't find much of use. Harvey had copies of scripts for all the roles he was coaching. All of them were minor ones such as "Townsman Number Two" and "Man in Stable." Rummaging through his desk drawers, I found several empty bottles of whiskey, two full bottles of vodka, and a hip flask filled with something that smelled like paint thinner. Perhaps it was paint thinner.

I spent my entire working life around soldiers

and thugs, and if there's one thing soldiers and thugs know how to do, it's drink. I've learned as many cures for hangovers as treatments for gunshot wounds.

I got to work.

FIVE

First things first. I put Harvey on his side so he didn't choke on his own vomit then went to brew some coffee at the little kitchenette the trailer had. Once I'd brewed up a strong pot, I poured the coffee into the container where the water was supposed to go, put in a new filter and grounds, and brewed it again.

A word of warning to the generally sober—do not try this at home. Brewing coffee from coffee instead of from water creates a nasty-smelling liquid more akin to motor oil than coffee. It will burn your throat, roil your stomach, and send razors through your gut.

It will wake you up, though.

Once I was done, I propped Harvey into a sitting position with his back against the wall (I was not going to risk bringing on an attack of sciatica by trying to get him into a chair) and poured some of the coffee down his throat.

I was rewarded by him sputtering, coughing, then sending a plume of twice-brewed coffee into my face.

I smacked him quite hard on the face several times. To wake him up. Really.

Harvey mumbled and slumped a little bit. I held up his chin and poured some more coffee down his throat.

He swallowed it this time, mostly because I had clamped his mouth shut and the liquid had nowhere else to go.

Once I felt satisfied he had swallowed, I poured some more down the hatch and clamped his mouth shut. Wait. Repeat.

After I'd given him about half the pot, I let him be. I sat on the chair to one side of him, to avoid any nasty surprises if his stomach decided to reject my concoction, and waited.

He muttered, rocked his head back and forth, and rubbed his hand weakly along his face before letting it fall back to his side.

"I wish I killed him," he mumbled.

I blinked, unsure if I had heard correctly. It couldn't be this easy, could it?

"I wish I killed him," he mumbled again. "Bastard deserves to die. I wish I had blown up that overrated piece of dirt."

He didn't use the word "dirt." I won't repeat what he actually said.

Then he mumbled something incoherent, let out a deafening belch, and opened his eyes. They were glazed and bloodshot and stared at the wall opposite him. "Piece of dirt," he repeated.

Once again, "dirt" was not the word.

"PIECE OF DIRT. THAT WAS MY DAMN GIRL. I'LL KILL THE FINK!"

Okay, that was a poor translation. Allow me to try again.

"PIECE OF BLEEP. THAT WAS MY BLEEPING GIRL. I'LL KILL THE BLEEEEP!"

That's better. Truer to the original while remaining printable.

He rocked his head back and forth.

"Bleep," he mumbled.

"Don't be vulgar," I scolded him.

"Huh?"

His head turned to follow the sound of my voice but got it wrong, so he ended up looking in the opposite direction.

"I'm over here," I said. I'm helpful that way.

He looked my direction.

"Who the bleep are you?"

"I'm Old Widow Margaret Goode, and I would ask you not to use the word 'bleep' in my presence. Don't use 'bleep,' 'bleep,' 'bleep,' or 'bleep' either. It shows a lack of imagination."

"If I had any bleeping imagination, I'd be a scriptwriter or a director instead of working this bleeping job."

I was getting tired of all the bleeping and felt tempted to give him a karate kick to the face. That would quiet him down. But I had to find out if he was serious about this killing business. If he was, case solved. If not, I still needed an acting coach.

His bleary eyes tried to focus on me.

"I thought you were dead," he said.

"I'm her replacement."

"Oh. Don't die. It's very inconvenient."

"I have no intention of dying for quite some time."

He looked around.

"Have you seen a bottle around here?" he asked.

"No, but I believe they're serving drinks at Cliff Armstrong's wake."

Those bleary eyes lit up like a pair of brake lights.

"The bleeper is finally dead? Thank God! They

got it right this time. Poor Bert, dying for a piece of bleep like that. He was a bleeping great guy."

"Who killed Bert?"

"Huh? How the bleep should I know? Some bleeping idiot, I suppose. Got the wrong bleeping guy."

I bit my lip. Harvey's face was wide open and easy to read. This man was too drunk to hide his guilt. He really didn't know. Just my bleeping luck.

He tried to get up, arms and legs flailing for a moment before he finally got them coordinated. By instinct, he went to the steaming coffee pot and drained the rest.

"Eeew." He made a face. "What the bleep is this?"

"Coffee brewed from coffee instead of water. Guaranteed wakeup call."

Harvey nodded in appreciation, tried to tuck in his shirt and only managed to tuck it between his belt and his pants, let out another belch, and looked at me. "Shall we get to work?"

"Are you up for it?" I asked dubiously.

He started to brew some more coffee. "Sure."

As he went through the motions, I could see a look of despair on his face. Not the usual pained look of your typical hangover, but proper angst. No doubt because of what had led him on the bender in the first place, although I had the impression that it didn't take much with him.

"Want to talk about it?" I asked.

"Bleeping Cliff Armstrong!" he yelled then added quietly, "Stole my girl."

"Your girl?"

"Tavern Wench Number Two. What a babe. Couldn't believe she fell for me or at least the bleep pretended to. Just did it so she could get to a party with Cliff Armstrong. As soon as she did, she ditched me and hopped into bed, the bleep."

"Just because she slept with a movie star doesn't mean she's a bleep."

"A bleep is a bleep. Would you have done that? No, because you're not a bleep. Of course you're too old to be a bleep, but even when you were younger, I bet you weren't a bleep."

"Please stop saying bleep. You're getting me to say it too."

"Whatever," he shrugged. He looked at me suspiciously. "Cliff Armstrong isn't really dead, is he?"

"No. Should he be?"

Harvey Miller slumped. "Yeah. That bleeping bleeper deserves to get it. Bert was a decent guy. Can't believe he got it instead."

"I was there when he got blown up. Such a terrible tragedy."

Harvey nodded. "That's Cliff Armstrong for you. He's like a bulldozer in a china shop, leaves a path of destruction in his wake and keeps on smiling for the cameras."

"But killing him seems a bit extreme."

"Ha! You must be new. All the egos in this business? Everyone, simply everyone wants to kill Cliff Armstrong. He's always stealing people's women or making people feel small. Thinks he's God's gift to acting."

I remembered how that crewmember had tried to stop him from coming over to greet the crowd. Cliff Armstrong had actually bared his teeth at the man. Was that his true nature? Big egos tended to be fragile egos, and if he was clashing with everyone on the set, I could see how he'd make a lot of enemies.

But enough to blow him up in front of everybody? Surely that would take more than a rude word or a stolen girlfriend.

Considering the state in which I found him, Harvey came around remarkably quickly. He shambled over to the desk, found a master copy of the script, and opened right to my first scene.

"Do you have all this memorized?" I asked.

"Of course. I know every beeping role in this bleeping picture, not that anyone gives me any credit. I'm at the bottom of this steaming bleep pile. Now, you look over those lines for a bit. I'll play the other roles and get you into character."

As I muttered my lines to myself, trying to memorize them and put some life into the words, Harvey made a phone call. I perked my ears. I've always listened in on other people's conversations. A bad habit, I know, but it's something you pick up, working for the CIA, and it's given me the most interesting life.

I was sure interested in what I heard next.

"Yeah, sure, I'll get her up to speed. You need her for dress rehearsal at seven tonight? No problem."

My heart did a little flip-flop. It was already two in the afternoon.

When he got off the phone I looked at him. "Did I hear that correctly? I'm supposed to do a dress rehearsal in less than five hours?"

"Yup," Harvey said, opening the desk drawer that contained all the bottles. He started clanking around, looking for one that wasn't empty. I slammed it shut.

"Ow!" he said, putting his fingers in his mouth.

"Stay sober. I need to do this right," I told him.

Because if I get fired, I'll never be able to solve this case and keep my favorite actor from being killed, I added silently.

I flipped through my three scenes. One was with the British officer in my house. Another had me sneaking away from my house and into the camp and had no dialog. In the third, I was warning Cliff Armstrong in the camp.

"Which one are we rehearsing tonight?" I asked.

"All three."

"Oh, Lord."

Then I realized something. All took place at night. All took place around soldiers. It would be dark, and there would be guns everywhere.

A perfect combination for murder.

SIX

Despite his potty mouth and his raging alcoholism, Harvey turned out to be quite good at what he did. The little fellow helped me learn the lines and set to work making me say them in a natural manner. He was brilliant with the other parts, putting on a posh English accent laced with evil when playing the British officer then giving me a vivid account of the dark forest I had to sneak through to get to the rebel camp. He offered an endless string of useful tips as I practiced my look of nervousness and the movements I had to do to get through the underbrush. Then he came on with an excellent imitation of Cliff Armstrong and played his part while I practiced my big scene.

His calm instruction, albeit peppered with belches and bleeps, calmed my nerves and got me into character. It was really quite a simple character, a stereotype really. Old Widow Margaret Goode had no past, no backstory, no family, no existence outside this movie. She didn't need one. She was the salt of the Earth who saw injustice and felt a patriotic stirring flutter in her aged heart. Although fearful of what the evil British officer might do to her, she braved the dark forest to bring a warning about the imminent attack to Cliff Armstrong, or "General John T. Slaughter" as he was known in this movie.

A minor role, but as Harvey explained to me, it was an important one.

"You see—*BELCH*—this movie, like all blockbusters, aims to appeal to everyone. That little bleep in the next trailer is to bring the kids in. There's a token black actor playing one of Cliff Armstrong's soldiers to get the blacks in. No mention of slavery, of course. That would be inconvenient. This is Hollywood, not history. Gwendolyn Parker plays the romantic lead. She's there to draw in the guys to look at her and for the girls to dream of being in her place. Your character draws in the old people."

"Wouldn't everyone come to this movie anyway, just because Cliff Armstrong is in it?"

Harvey made a face. "Sure, everyone loves that bleeping bleep. And, yeah, he's what gets butts in seats, to use an industry phrase, but if you want to keep people coming back, they have to relate to the picture. They have to put themselves in it somehow. We even worked in a gay angle."

"Really?"

"Oh yeah, Cliff Armstrong is a major attraction for gay guys. So we have this one minuteman, kind of a pretty boy, but a good fighter. He doesn't get many lines, but he's an officer, so he's in a lot of scenes with Cliff Armstrong. Looks at him a lot from the background. There's this one scene where the minutemen are marching along a country lane, and these sexy farm girls come out and wave their handkerchiefs at the guys. Really hot girls. Casting did great with them. Then the camera cuts to the guys marching along. Every one of them is grinning at the girls and waving except for that one officer, who is looking right at Cliff Armstrong."

"Will anyone even notice?"

"You wouldn't notice. Your friends won't notice, but the gays sure will notice, and they'll be cheering that minuteman until he heroically dies taking a bullet for his studly general."

"Won't the gay fans be disappointed?"

"Sure, they'll be bawling into their tissues, but it's cathartic. They'll love every minute of it. And when the next Cliff Armstrong movie comes out, they'll come back for more."

"I didn't realize so much thought went into these things."

"Oh, bleep yeah. It's all gotten a bit chaotic, though, what with the casting director off getting a nip and tuck, and Cliff Armstrong acting like his usual bleeping self, and the original Old Widow Margaret Goode dying on us, and then an attempted murder on the set."

"Who do you think did it?" I asked. Now that Harvey was more sober, maybe he would have some answers.

To my disappointment, he only shook his head. "Wish I knew so I could give the guy a bleeping medal. I only hope he's more successful next time. Oh, hey, it's almost seven. We gotta get you to rehearsal. Now, don't worry. I'll be with you every step of the way."

With that, he opened the desk drawer and pulled out a bottle of vodka before I could stop him.

"Put that away. You've had enough for one night!"

"Not a chance," he said between gulps. "If some idiot is trying to kill Cliff Armstrong and I gotta stand on the same set as him, I'm going to need some liquid courage. I don't want to get blown up like Bert, at least not while I'm sober."

That sobered me up considerably. For a while, as I was playing my part and learning my lines, I had forgotten the danger, but now the reality of my situation came back to me. Cliff Armstrong was a walking target, and anyone who got near him stood in the crosshairs too. Poor old Bert was proof of that.

Harvey finished off the bottle, wiped his mouth with the back of his hand, let out a deep-throated belch, and said, "Walk this way," as he stumbled out of the trailer.

"To walk that way, I'd have to be as drunk as you are," I said.

"Har har."

He wove his way between the trailers toward a brightly lit set I could see at the end of the road.

"We're doing the scene with Cliff Armstrong first," Harvey said, slurring his words. "Remember your lines?"

"Yes." There weren't very many of them.

"Good. You're a quick study. The only way to get ahead in Hollywood is to be smart and pay attention."

At this point, Harvey tripped over an electrical cable and landed flat on his face.

"Oh bleep! What bleeping bleep left that bleeping cord there? BLEEP!"

A couple of teamsters standing nearby held their bellies and laughed.

"Stand up and stop bleeping," I said. "You're embarrassing me."

He managed to get to his feet and not have any further pratfalls before making it to the set, which stood in a small grassy area near the street.

The set was brilliantly illuminated, making the street, which was well lit itself, seem like the darkest night in comparison.

Several spotlights, backed by big reflective sheets that looked like giant parasols, focused on the front of a tent and a campfire. A few crudely made wooden chairs stood around it, and several extras in minutemen uniforms milled around, drinking coffee out of Styrofoam cups, or stood still as makeup artists put the final touches on their faces. As I entered the circle of light, one of the makeup artists swooped in on me.

"Sit down on that stool over there," the young woman ordered. "You're not old enough."

"I've never been told that before."

"Please don't talk. It will slow down my work."

So, I sat there in silence as she put all sorts of unidentifiable gunk on my face. The only thing I could move was my eyes, and I took in as much of the situation as I could.

During my time as a field operative, I had learned to look at a location and pick out its dangers. It's something that comes with the job, and if you don't learn it quick, you're dead.

What I was seeing was an ambusher's paradise.

Sitting on the set, with all the lights focused on us, we couldn't see anyone around us. The rest of the world might as well have not existed. Someone could have been standing five feet from me with a bazooka, and I wouldn't have spotted them. We were exposed not only from the street around us but from the rooftops of the buildings on either side of the street. Plus, there were so many people bustling around no one was paying any attention to anyone else. An assassin could easily slip in and do their work.

My nervousness increased when Cliff Armstrong strode onto the set, flanked by a pair of tough guys who I suppose were meant to be body-guards. The problem was, they stepped into the circle of light and were just as blind to their surroundings as the rest of us.

Amateurs.

Cliff snatched a script from one of the minutemen who was doing some last-minute practicing with his lines and read through the pages. The minuteman glared at the movie star's back for a moment before slinking off.

Just as the makeup person put the finishing touches on me, Cliff Armstrong bawled, "So where's this old widow chick? Didn't she die or something?"

"We got a new one, Mr. Armstrong," Harvey said.

"Oh hey, Harvey, glad to see you upright for a change," Cliff Armstrong said.

I moved over to where my film hero, and now my coworker, stood. I felt like I was floating on air. Well, floating on air on a malfunctioning hovercraft. I shook so much from nerves that I could barely walk straight.

Cliff Armstrong frowned at me then frowned at Harvey. "You been getting the actors drunk too? Nice going, Harvey."

"I'm not drunk, just a little nervous. It's my first time."

Cliff grinned. The light gleamed off his teeth. "I've heard that one before."

I nearly fell over. "I mean my first time on camera."

"I know what you mean," he said with a dismissive wave. Then he peered at me, trying to see my features under the heavy makeup.

"Heeey, aren't you one half of that old couple I met yesterday?"

I was shocked he remembered. He must have said hello to a hundred people. "Well, Octavian and I are just dating."

"So, you're a fan?" he seemed to be both surprised and disappointed. "What are you doing coming over to the Dark Side?"

He definitely said that with capital letters. I tried to remember if he had been in any of the *Star Wars* movies, but there had been so many of them lately I had lost track.

"You consider acting something evil?" I asked.

Cliff Armstrong grunted. "Take my advice, and get out of this lousy career as quickly as you can."

"Quiet on the set!" Vance Randolph's voice shouted from somewhere in the darkness. "Let's get this scene done. Actors, take your places."

Harvey moved me over to the edge of the set, from where I was supposed to hurry over to General John T. Slaughter and his men as they sat around the campfire. Cliff Armstrong and the others took their places, the star sitting in a camp chair in front of the fire, the others arranged around him. A boom mic moved directly over Cliff Armstrong.

"Move that mic up a bit. It's still in the shot," one of the cameramen said.

The mic, on the end of a long steel pole, moved up a foot.

"That's good," the cameraman said.

"Lights!" the director shouted.

My heart started to pound. Suddenly I forgot every one of my lines.

The lights dimmed and changed color in imitation of flickering firelight. That struck me as odd, since there was a perfectly good real fire right in front of them. I suppose that wasn't enough to make it look like a real fire on camera.

I stopped thinking about that and wondered how the heck I was going to look like a real actress on camera.

"Camera one, how is your shot?" Vance Randolph asked.

"Good."

"Camera two?"

"Good."

"Camera three?"

"Old Widow Margaret Goode needs to move half a step to the left."

I leaped like I had just been electrocuted. It was

only when the cameraman spoke that I noticed a camera pointing directly at me.

"Move half a step to the left. We don't have all day!" Vance Randolph barked.

Meekly I took a little step to the left. I felt woozy and looked heavenward. Not that I thought God would help me out of this mess, He certainly had better things to do, but because it was the only direction where I couldn't see cameras or directors or actors or all this alien nonsense surrounding me.

Except for the boom mic. It hovered in the air above the actors. Suddenly it rose up, quickly extending. I looked at it curiously. Wouldn't it be too high to catch the sound of their voices? Plus the director hadn't ordered it to be raised.

Vance Randolph noticed it too. "Hey, sound. What are you doing?" he demanded.

Suddenly it became sickeningly clear what he was doing.

"Look out!" I shouted.

The boom mic dropped, its heavy steel pole flashing down on the heads of the actors below.

SEVEN

Cliff Armstrong let out a yelp and threw himself on the ground. The man standing next to him wasn't so lucky. The boom smacked him right on the top of the head with a sickening crunch, and he collapsed like a house of cards. The boom hit the chair where Cliff Armstrong had been sitting a moment before and shivered, making a strange whining metallic sound as its entire length wobbled. The other actors, most of whom had been missed by inches, leaped back a moment later or simply stood in shock, staring at the dead man next to the campfire.

And he was quite obviously dead. Blood poured from his head, which was caved in right along the top.

Everyone ran onto the set, a babble of voices

drowning out any sense to the situation.

Everyone but me, that is. I ran to where the boom mic operator had been standing.

I found him lying on the ground unconscious. The boom mic, which was on a sort of weighted stand to keep it steady, had a clamp to lock the boom in place. That had been flicked open.

I saw all this in an instant. The next moment, I heard a woman holding a clipboard shout, "He went that way!"

She pointed off the set toward the tangle of trailers. I didn't see anyone.

"Who?" I demanded.

"The guy who hit Clyde. I was standing here, waiting to prompt you on your lines, when someone walked up behind Clyde, knocked him over the head with a wrench, extended the boom, and flipped the catch!"

I barely heard that last part, because I was already running in the direction the script girl had pointed.

Well, "running."

My knees aren't what they used to be. Neither are my ankles. Every now and then my sciatica acts up, and I get tired far more easily than I used to. I can't even see the sights on my nine-millimeter automatic pistol without my reading glasses. That didn't matter, because I didn't have my gun with me anyway.

It's a bit of a cheat that I had been in prime physical health all my life only to decay so quickly by age seventy. I know many people who had worked office jobs and only went to the gym on weekends who were in better shape than me now. The truth is, I overdid it. All those fifty-mile marches with hundred-pound packs took their toll. All those nights sleeping out in the rain, all those days slogging through the desert, all those times I was on the receiving end of bullets or fists or a bronze bust of Ronald Reagan used as a club (don't ask) had finally caught up to me. My body had been getting weaker even when it seemed at its strongest, and now I had to pay the price. The only thing left in one hundred percent working order was my mind. At least the Great CIA Director in the Sky hadn't taken that from me.

As I hurried through the maze of trailers, that mind was working overtime.

I had learned something very important about the killer, in fact a few things.

First, he was a man. At least if that script girl had seen correctly. I'd have to speak with her more later.

Second, he was desperate. He was so intent on

killing Cliff Armstrong that he didn't mind getting caught. Both times he had tried to kill the movie star had been when lots of other people had been around. That meant he didn't care about getting caught, although he certainly wanted to make sure that he killed Cliff Armstrong first, hence this chase.

Third, he didn't care if other people got killed. The first time with Bert was an honest mistake. It should have been Cliff Armstrong running through that field. Many potential murderers aren't true killers, and it takes a lot to push them over the edge. If they kill an innocent bystander by accident, they will be so remorseful they either turn themselves in to the police or stop trying to kill the original target. This killer had tried again the very next day and in a crowd of people who were bound to get hurt even if he did succeed.

All that flickered through my mind as I hurried between two large trailers, their roofs adorned with giant satellite dishes.

I stopped for a moment, unsure of myself. After rushing out of the light and crowd of the set, this area looked dark and abandoned by comparison.

No, not quite abandoned. I heard a door slam shut on the other side of the trailer to my left.

Running around the front of the trailer, I came

across another row of trailers. This place was a veritable town of trailers. One was marked "Costume C." The one just behind was marked "Costume B." I came around the corner just in time to see a figure duck between them.

I pursued. I really shouldn't have, considering that I was no longer deadly in hand-to-hand combat, but old habits died hard.

Old instincts died hard too, and just as I got close to the back of the Costume C trailer, they told me to take care.

I stopped. Listened. Was that the faint sound of breathing I heard? It was hard to tell, because the hubbub over at the set hadn't died down. In fact, it had grown louder as more people gathered around. The curious flock to murder scenes and car crashes —any tragedy, really—like flies flock to bleep.

Oh dear, Harvey was getting to me.

I crouched down, wincing as one of my knees popped. I hoped the killer hadn't heard. To me, it sounded like a pistol shot.

I looked beneath the truck, and as I suspected, a pair of feet stood just around the corner of the truck. No doubt further up there was a pair of hands gripping that wrench, ready to smack the annoying little old lady who had dared to pursue him.

White tennis shoes, big enough that they were almost certainly a man's. Blue jeans. That's all I could see.

What I couldn't tell was why he wasn't a mile away by now. I am not exactly a fast runner these days, and he had a good head start on me.

The slamming door. He had gone into Costume Trailer C for some reason. He hadn't stayed long, but he had risked getting caught so he could go in there.

Why?

First things first, I needed to grab this guy, or at least get a good look at him. I tiptoed back the way I came so I could come at him from the front of the trailer. The light was good enough that I would get a decent look at him.

No such luck.

"She said he went this way!" someone shouted from not far off. This was followed by the sound of stomping feet.

By the time I got around the costume trailer, the killer had disappeared.

Cliff Armstrong's two bodyguards blundered into view. They looked around with blank expressions on their faces for a moment then ran off in a random direction.

I sighed in frustration. Only dumb luck would

send them on the killer's route, and I do mean dumb.

Since no one else was around for the moment, I took a look inside Costume Trailer C.

I could have groaned with despair when I opened the door.

It was stuffed with uniforms. Not costumes, but uniforms. Reflective jackets for road crews, white clothing for the caterers, green jumpsuits I'd seen the cleanup crews wearing, hardhats, kneepads, gloves, everything a small mobile town like this film crew would need.

The perfect place for a killer to come do a quick change and blend with the film crew. Even if he had only had a minute to spare in this place, he could have chosen between a dozen different uniforms. He could look like anyone by now.

Had he walked off as a cook? An electrician? It was impossible to say. It did teach me one thing, though, and that was the killer was familiar with the layout of the film set. He had known exactly where to go to get his getaway disguise.

He was working on this film.

That narrowed it down to a couple hundred people.

It was a start, I suppose.

EIGHT

The next day I called Grimal. The police chief did not sound happy to hear from me, but he knew that he couldn't avoid this conversation. The poor fellow had probably been dreading it all morning.

"What do you want?" he groaned.

"Manners," I chided him. "And you know very well what I want."

"I spoke with the script girl," he said. "Mary Ellworth. She was the only one who got a clear look at the killer. White male, medium build, not too young or too old, wearing a black hooded sweatshirt with a red logo on the front."

"What was the logo?"

"She didn't see. She only saw him for a moment. You know how witnesses can be."

I nodded. Most people make terrible witnesses.

They aren't paying attention until the actual crime takes place, and then they're so shocked that the whole thing is a blur. Little Mary Ellworth had actually done comparatively well.

"Oh, she did say the logo seemed familiar," Grimal added.

"Familiar how?"

"She can't say. She's been racking her brains about it but can't figure it out. She said she'd call if anything jogged her memory."

I didn't put much hope in that. Most people, even intelligent people who haven't just witnessed a murder, have faulty memories. Scientists say that our memories aren't imprinted in our brain like some sort of picture but rather are reconstructed from bits and pieces. That means a lot of embellishment and filling in the blanks occurs. And each time a memory is recalled, it gets a little further from the original. You can see this for yourself by conducting a simple experiment. Recall a favorite scene from a movie that you haven't watched in a while, a scene that you've replayed in your head many times. You think you know who does what and exactly what all the actors said? Now watch that scene again, and you'll see that you've made quite a few little mistakes in your recollection. This isn't so important with a movie, but it can literally be a matter of life or death in a case like this.

"Why didn't she shout when the murderer knocked Clyde the boom man over the head?" I asked.

"She choked up with fear. Not an unusual reaction."

"A convenient one too."

"I'm surprised you didn't grill her yourself." Grimal sounded churlish.

"I didn't want to blow my cover."

"Your cover?" Grimal posed this as a question. One of those questions you don't want the answer to but feel compelled to ask anyway, like "does this dress make me look fat?"

"I got a job as an extra. Old Widow Margaret Goode, to be exact."

"You're going to be in the movie." His voice came out flat.

"Yes."

"With Cliff Armstrong."

"Yes."

"Are you in scenes with him?"

"One. I was present when the boom mic came down." I proceeded to tell him all I saw that night, which didn't amount to much.

"But that puts you in danger," Grimal said after

I had finished. I couldn't tell if he was worried I'd get killed on his watch and he'd get in trouble with the CIA or if he was hoping I'd get killed on his watch and he'd be free of me.

"It's the perfect way to find the killer," I said, feeling rather defensive. This whole thing really wasn't any of my business. Retirement doesn't sit well with me, though.

"You know these idiots are going to continue with the picture? After two murders on the set?" He sounded exasperated. I could tell he just wanted this whole problem to go away and leave him alone. He felt the same about me.

"That doesn't surprise me. Film people are … odd. They have their own little community, a rather pathetic and divided community, and yet somehow it all comes together, and these pictures get made. I'm finding the whole experience quite educational."

"So am I. I'm learning just how stupid Hollywood people are, and I'm learning that voting for our governor in the last election was the dumbest thing I ever did."

"Oh, I wouldn't say that."

Grimal missed the point. "I got another call from him this morning, right after a bunch of panicky calls from California lawyers telling me not to try to shut down the set. The governor told me the same thing. Ordered me, really. He said, 'The show must go on.' Can you believe it? You know, these guys don't give a damn about Cliff Armstrong. They just want to get their picture made. When I pointed out to one of those lawyers that they wouldn't have a movie if their star got killed, he told me that they had enough footage of him that they could splice him into scenes using CGI. They've done it before when actors have died."

"And no doubt Cliff Armstrong's final movie would be the biggest blockbuster yet," I said.

The significance of my own words took a moment to sink in. Yes, it would make the film quite profitable, wouldn't it? It seemed everyone from Harvey all the way up to Vance Randolph were thoroughly sick of dealing with Cliff Armstrong but were professionally invested in this film. If the star died, that would relieve them of a burden, and at the same time they'd have the notoriety of having been involved in perhaps the biggest grossing movie of all time. Everyone's careers would prosper.

That widened the circle of suspects considerably. I could not dismiss the possibility that the killer may not have a personal motive but may have been hired by someone to do their dirty work. That person could be one of those California producers.

But perhaps that didn't fit so well. The killer was too determined, too unconcerned about his own ultimate safety, to be a hired man. Even if someone had put him up to it, the killer was still working from his own motivations. Could there be a conspiracy?

I still had too many questions, but some of the pieces of the puzzle were beginning to appear. I hadn't been able to put them together yet, but at least I was seeing the hint of an overall pattern. That always made me feel tingly inside. Not as tingly as meeting Cliff Armstrong but a decent second.

"Grimal, look into the insurance status of this movie and of Cliff Armstrong."

"Why?"

I rolled my eyes. This guy was clearly in over his head. "Because someone might reap a big profit if their star dies."

"Oh."

"You hadn't thought of that, had you?"

Yes, that was nasty, but I do deserve a little bit of fun, don't I?

"It was on my list of things to do," he mumbled.

It sure is now, I thought.

"The governor at least gave us something," the police chief said.

"What's that?"

"He's given me twenty plainclothes police officers from other districts to help out. I've gotten them jobs as extras and caterers."

"And who in the crew knows they're cops?"

Long silence. I shook my head.

I heard Grimal shift in his seat.

"Well, we told the assistant casting manager, a Ms. Russo. And we had to tell the head of the catering company, but he's local. No way he's a suspect."

"Anyone else?"

"We told them to keep mum."

"Like that ever happens."

People thought being involved in a police case was exciting. They couldn't help blabbing to friends and family, and those people blabbed to other people, and soon everyone knew.

Hopefully the news wouldn't spread too quickly. The killer seemed in a hurry, so perhaps he'd strike before he heard that the police had infiltrated the set, although if he had any brains, he must have realized that would happen sooner rather than later.

"So, who was the victim last night?" I asked. I

hadn't lingered after the murder. Filming was cut off for the night, and most of us were told to go home.

"Randy Bowen. Minor character actor. Had a couple of lines in this film. So far we've found no reason for him to be targeted. It looks like he was just in the wrong place at the wrong time."

"He was. You know, come to think of it, he was standing right next to Cliff Armstrong and in line with the boom mic. Either the killer miscalculated, or he didn't care that Randy would be hit by the metal pole too."

Grimal groaned. A groaning Grimal had become part of the soundtrack to my life. "Great. That's just dandy. So, we have a psycho killer on our hands."

"Oh, I'm not sure he's a psychopath. He just doesn't care if innocent people get killed."

"Sounds like a psychopath to me. They can be devious and meticulous, you know. This guy doesn't seem to care if he gets away with it as long as he gets it done. Oh, and we're keeping the killing under wraps. It hasn't leaked out to the press yet, and if it does, we're calling it an accident. The press is already having a field day with that stuntman getting blown up. We don't need any journalists sniffing around."

"Indeed. Any more news for me?" I asked.

"No." He sounded like a chastened schoolchild who had just brought home a bad report card. He knew I had just given him a D- for police work.

I hung up without saying goodbye. It's what they did in movies, after all. Ever notice that? Very unrealistic.

Checking my watch, I saw I had just enough time to feed Dandelion, who had been feeling rather neglected the past two days, and head to the set. I was supposed to film that scene today after the rather rude interruption we had experienced the previous evening.

Poor Octavian. He had called that morning, asking if I wanted to go to lunch. I had made excuses. I didn't want to tell him I had a date with Cliff Armstrong instead.

I had been instructed to go to a certain part of the set that was called the "Extras Corral," a rather demeaning name for a large open area where the extras were supposed to gather before being herded to their next scene. Harvey had told me I was going to be in some group shots of the townspeople.

Parking was a nightmare, and I had to leave my car two blocks away (extras didn't get reserved parking) and walk. Parking at a strip mall dressed as an old widow from the American Revolution was a new thing for me, but no one batted an eyelid. That sort of thing had become a common sight in Cheerville already.

When I got to the Extras Corral and looked at the cattle—I mean, extras—I had the shock of my life.

My son Frederick and my grandson Martin were there, dressed in eighteenth-century clothing.

"What are you doing here?" we asked in unison. Given our costumes, the answer was obvious. It was sort of like asking "Are you okay?" to someone who had just fallen down the stairs. Ridiculous, but what else can you say?

"We've been hired as extras." My son grinned. "And you did too?"

I nodded.

"We're going to be in a Cliff Armstrong movie! This is the best summer vacation ever!" Martin shouted, jumping up and down. He was thirteen and tried to act the part of a cool teenager most of time, but the child he still half was came out when he got excited.

I smiled at him and tried to hide my worry. This set had become a warzone, and now two of my favorite people in the world were going to be hanging out here?

"What about Alicia?" I asked after my daughter-in-law.

Martin made a face. "Mom says she's too busy. She's got some boring meeting in the city tomorrow."

Alicia is a leading scientist and one of the most driven people I have ever met. I had always worried that her overworking would be bad for her health. Now it might actually save her life.

On the far side of the lot, an older man stepped onto a platform and addressed us through a megaphone.

"Okay, everyone to the front of the church. We're filming the final scene, the wedding shot where General Slaughter and Liberty Smith come out of the church and the townspeople cheer. Old Widow Goode, wherever you are, get over here. You're standing right next to the stairs with the minutemen."

"That would be me," I told my family with a smile. They gaped in awe.

I moved away, and my smile died. Great, right in the firing line again.

The next two hours were excruciating. We did that shot a dozen times, with Cliff Armstrong and Gwendolyn Parker coming out arm in arm while we threw rice at the newlyweds and the towns-people stood on the village green and cheered.

Yes, rice. Did they have rice in the American colonies? Somehow I don't think so. But I wasn't thinking about historical accuracy at that point.

I shuddered when I saw Frederick and Martin standing right next to the chewed-up earth where Bert had been killed. The crew had covered it over, of course, but I could still see the rough area where they had put new turf and some scorch marks on the surrounding grass. A man had died there, blown apart by a determined killer, and now my precious family stood on the same spot.

My gaze roved across the crowd, looking for anyone acting suspiciously.

But there were so many people around, a sea of faces, all intently staring at us.

Somewhere, I knew, the killer was among them. Watching.

NINE

But the killer did not strike. We finished the shot, and the extras were told to go home. Harvey pushed his way through the crowd of minutemen and told me to stay put. They'd be setting up the campfire shot, and I was still needed.

"But that's a night scene, and it's broad daylight," I said.

Harvey threw his arms wide, inadvertently knocking the tricorne off the nearest minuteman. "Welcome to the magic of movies."

"Smells to me like you're enjoying the magic of vodka."

"It's called liquid courage, and I'm feeling brave."

"It's going to be at least an hour for them to set

up," one of the minutemen told me. "Let's go get lunch. Harvey, you coming?"

"I got lunch in my trailer."

"Any food in that lunch?" the minuteman asked with a grin.

"Go bleep yourself," he grumbled as he walked away.

My nerves had left me without an appetite, but this would be a good opportunity to interview the actors playing the minutemen. They had been at the murder scene the night before and knew the poor fellow who had been killed.

So I accompanied a bunch of strapping young men to lunch. There are worse ways to spend my time.

The catering truck was the size of a touring bus and opened up on the side to turn into an open-air cafeteria. We walked along with plastic trays and picked whatever we wanted while the catering staff bustled around behind the counter, cooking and adding more food to the selection. It was a bit like being back in school again, except there were vegan, gluten-free, organic, and cruelty-free options. This was Hollywood, after all.

We found a table under a large awning and sat, surrounded by British soldiers, bit players in the eighteenth-century civilian garb of farmers and tavern wenches, and a few technical people not in costume.

"This your first movie?" one of the minutemen asked.

"Yes, how can you tell?"

"You keep looking around you like you're in the middle of a three-ring circus," another said.

"That's what it feels like," I admitted.

They laughed at that.

One grew serious. "Cliff Armstrong giving you any trouble?"

"He recognized me from the crowd of fans and seemed disappointed that I had joined the cast."

One of them nodded and chuckled. "He hates Hollywood and everyone involved in it."

"But it's made him rich and famous!" I objected.

"It's made him arrogant and insufferable," one of them snapped.

"Does no one like him?" I still hadn't gotten over the fact that my cinema hero had two sides to his personality.

"No one in the business," one of the minutemen grumbled. He was the handsomest of them all, a bit of a pretty boy, and I wondered if this was the fellow Harvey had been talking about. "Cliff Armstrong is like Dr. Jekyll and Mr. Hyde.

When he's with his fans, he's great. That's because they feed his ego. When he's with people who have to have a professional relationship with him and demand to be treated equally, he can't handle it."

I shook my head like I was a shocked, innocent old lady. It's easy to get young people to underestimate you, especially young men. That often proved helpful because they told you things you might otherwise not hear. "I can't believe someone would want to murder him," I said.

"Lots of people would like to murder him," Pretty Boy said. Then he appeared to realize what he had just said and quickly added, "But whoever did this is crazy. He's killed two innocent people. This guy doesn't care who gets hurt. That makes him worse than the guy he's trying to kill. All Cliff Armstrong has ever done is beat someone up."

"What?" This time, I didn't have to feign my shock.

One of the minutemen raised a quietening hand, but Pretty Boy wouldn't be stopped.

"One of the CGI guys. They're everywhere these days. You used to get them only in science fiction pictures, but even historical films use them now. They erase electrical lines from the background and get rid of jet contrails and make crowds look bigger. So, this CGI guy, Lars Mollan, was working on *Race Against*

Death. One of the best guys in the business. Did great with all those crash scenes and explosions. But little special snowflake Cliff Armstrong didn't like how Lars lit him. Made a big fuss and insulted the guy in front of everybody. He could have just asked for some simple changes, but he completely blew his top, as usual. But he's the star, so he got his way, as usual."

"Not quite," one of the minutemen chuckled.

Pretty Boy grinned. "Yeah. Lars made the changes all right but added some changes of his own. In one scene, Cliff Armstrong is in a swimming pool wearing Speedos—"

"I remember that scene," I said with a sigh. Everyone looked at me like I'd just stepped out of a flying saucer. Old ladies aren't supposed to have desires.

Pretty Boy gave a little shudder and went on. "So, in one of the scenes, he did a bit of … altering. Reduced his bulge to something a grade-schooler would be ashamed of. No one in the editing room noticed it, and it made it into the theaters."

Everyone laughed. Except me. I had a feeling I was getting somewhere.

"But Cliff Armstrong noticed and beat him up?" I asked.

Pretty Boy made a face. "That he did. At a

nightclub. The producers managed to hush it up. It never made it into the press. There was a lawsuit, and Lars got a settlement that never made it into the papers, but everyone in the business saw the real Cliff Armstrong that night."

"I hope Mr. Mollan doesn't try to alter any bulges in this picture," I probed.

One of the minutemen grinned. "He's under close supervision."

Oh, so he was on the set. That's what I wanted to know.

Pretty Boy pulled up the cuff of his uniform to reveal a watch.

"Hey, it's about time we got going."

Everyone stood up.

"I'll join you boys in a moment," I said. "I just need to freshen up."

"Don't be long," one of them said. "The show must go on."

I ducked into one of the porta potties lining one side of the dining area, wrinkled my nose at the smell, and put in a call to Grimal.

"Do a background check on Lars Mollan. He's working in the CGI department. Also see if you can find out the terms of the settlement he made with Cliff Armstrong after they had a fight."

I hung up before he could say anything. I didn't have time to waste on him.

I was barely out of the porta potty when Harvey intercepted me.

"Come on. We got a tight schedule, and we're behind already!" He looked more sober than usual, meaning he was only slightly drunk. We hurried through the maze of trailers.

Just as we got to the set, I found another scene of confusion.

"Where's General Slaughter?" Vance Randolph's voice boomed through the megaphone. "Hey, where the hell is General Slaughter?"

Everyone looked around. Cliff Armstrong was nowhere to be seen.

"And he calls me unprofessional," Harvey grumbled.

I got a cold feeling in the pit of my stomach. Mary Ellworth, the script coach from the previous night, offered to check his trailer and hurried off. I followed.

"Stay here!" Harvey shouted at my back. I ignored him.

I managed not to lose Mary Ellworth in the crowd, and she led me straight to a large trailer set a little apart from the rest. Next to the door, which was shut, a sign displayed Cliff Armstrong's name in big gold lettering. In fact, it looked like they had used actual gold.

The script coach knocked timidly on the door. "Mr. Armstrong?"

I didn't hear a response as I came up behind her. She didn't notice me.

"Mr. Armstrong? We're ready to shoot."

A low mumble came from within. I could not tell if that was the star's voice or not.

Mary grew more insistent, knocking and repeating her words louder this time.

Something thumped on the inside of the door.

"Oh God, he's throwing things again," the script coach muttered. "I've had enough of this."

She turned to leave and noticed me standing there.

"These stars are nothing but big babies," she told me. "There's nothing you can do."

She walked off, not looking to see if I followed.

I paused. Was Cliff Armstrong really in a sulk, or was something else going on in there?

I looked around. The script coach was walking away, and for the moment, no one else was paying the trailer any attention, but I knew time was short. The director would send someone to fetch him soon. He might even come himself if his star wouldn't listen to an underling.

Luckily, I had come prepared. I pulled a set of lock picks out of my pocket and got to work on the door.

It proved ridiculously easy. I could have probably opened the flimsy little latch lock with a credit card.

I popped open the lock and paused again. I heard nothing but silence within. Had he heard me? I had picked the lock pretty quietly. Blundering into the trailer without my gun went against all my gut instincts. Sometimes, though, you have to just push ahead to get the job done.

Note to self: always go with your gut instincts.

As I opened the door, I felt a slight resistance. The door gave, but something was pulling against it.

I leaped to one side and hit the pavement just as the explosion went off.

In truth, calling it an explosion was a bit of an overstatement. There was a loud pop, a cracking sound, and some black gritty smoke poofed out of the doorway. I heard the unmistakable sound of metal shrapnel crack on the pavement.

But not much shrapnel. It sounded like a home-made bomb and not a very good one either.

I struggled to my feet, wincing in pain as my sciatica decided this was a good moment to warn me of my mortality, like I hadn't just been given enough of a reminder. Someone was screaming. I looked around and saw it was Mary Ellworth. She stood not far off, trembling from head to foot but otherwise unharmed. People were converging from all around.

I limped into the trailer. I had only a few seconds to check the crime scene before half the crew trampled all over it.

Waving my hand to disperse the last of the smoke, I peered inside.

And saw one of the strangest sights of my life.

TEN

Cliff Armstrong sat tied to a chair in the middle of the trailer. It was surreal to see him like that. I'd seen him tied up so many times on screen—to a chair, to the conveyor belt in a sawmill, to the outside of the International Space Station—but I had never seen him tied up in real life.

He did not look terribly heroic, and I did not think that he'd come up with a clever way to get out of those ropes and save the day.

Mostly because he looked drunk. He sat slumped in his bonds, head lolling to the side, his eyes trying to focus on me. As I entered, he mumbled something like, "Get out of here." At least that's what it sounded like.

I glanced around. The trailer was like a miniature mansion and dressing room rolled into one.

Cliff Armstrong was tied up in front of a makeup table. Various creams and powders were arrayed in front of a mirror encircled by lights. To one side sat a lounge chair with a miniature fridge next to it, an expensive-looking sound system, a flat-screen TV, and a hot tub. Yes, a hot tub. I had never seen a hot tub in a trailer before. Perhaps they're common these days. I don't know. I need to get out more.

Of more immediate concern was the home-made bomb attached by a tripwire to the door.

It was a small metal cylinder with a detonator fixed to one end. It had been set into place with two heavy blocks of wood on the side opposite that facing the door. Because of this, all the force of the explosion (caused by a small amount of black powder, judging from the smell of the smoke) had blown toward the door, peppering it and the pavement outside with fragments of the cylinder.

A crude bomb, unprofessionally made. And those thick wooden chocks had, intentionally or otherwise, made all the shrapnel shoot at me and not at Cliff Armstrong. An explosion will always take the path of least resistance.

I blinked, feeling a coldness in the pit of my stomach. Whoever had tied up the movie star had had a perfect opportunity to slit his throat without anyone seeing or hearing. Cliff Armstrong could be dead and the killer far away by now, but instead, he had rigged up this bomb to kill whoever had the nerve to come through the door.

Was he gunning for me personally? Had our little chase made him see me as a bigger threat to his plans than anyone else? If so, that didn't explain why the killer hadn't finished Cliff Armstrong off when he had the chance. Then he wouldn't have had to worry about me at all.

This didn't fit with the profile I had been making of the killer, that of a driven individual who didn't care about his personal safety as long as he managed to take out the movie star first. Now he was showing caution and playing a game of cat and mouse.

What had changed?

By this point, a whole crowd had assembled in front of the trailer, everyone peering inside. One fellow raised his phone to take a picture, only to have it slapped out of his hand by one of Cliff Armstrong's bodyguards. Yes, Tweedledee and Tweedledum had finally made their appearance.

"Where were you?" I demanded.

"Mr. Armstrong wanted his privacy," Tweedledee said, pushing his muscular bulk through the narrow door and accidentally kicking the cylinder, thereby disturbing a crime scene.

"You are bodyguards. You're not supposed to give your client privacy."

"And who are you?" Tweedledum demanded.

"Old Widow Margaret Goode. I came to find out why Cliff Armstrong hadn't shown up on the set."

"Can you prove that?" Tweedledum crowded me into a corner. I did not feel intimidated. He stood with his legs planted far apart so that he would appear even bigger than he was. That worked, but it also left him open to the kind of cheap shot that most men are eager to avoid.

The script coach came to my rescue. "I got here first. I was knocking on the door, and he didn't open up. As I was leaving, she opened the door to check on him, and the bomb went off."

Good thing she hadn't seen me pick the lock. That would have been hard to explain.

"Can you prove that?" Tweedledum demanded. Both of us rolled our eyes.

Tweedledee started untying Cliff Armstrong.

"Why is he drunk on the set? I thought he was a professional," I said. All my lovely myths about Hollywood and stardom were falling away one by one. The magic of the movies didn't seem so magical anymore.

"He's not drunk. He doesn't drink," Tweedledee

said with the smug satisfaction of someone who thought he had private access to the great.

"Has he been drugged?" the script coach asked. She stood at the doorway, peering in. She hadn't dared enter. That was fine, because standing where she was, she served the purpose of blocking the doorway from the rest of the gaping crowd.

"Looks like Rohypnol," the bodyguard said, loosening the last of the bonds. "I used to work in a nightclub in the city. I saw this a lot."

Rohypnol was a tranquilizer, better known as the "date-rape drug." You put a little of the powder in someone's drink, and it incapacitates them. They don't go totally unconscious, but they can't resist and have no recollection of what happened when they recover.

"Must have been in that orange juice," Tweedledee said, pointing to a half-empty glass on the makeup table. "Good thing he didn't have the whole thing, or he'd be completely out of it." He crouched so he could look the movie star in the eye and raised his voice. "Mr. Armstrong, when did you drink the orange juice?"

Cliff Armstrong mumbled something. The bodyguard repeated the question.

"About half an hour ago," Cliff Armstrong

managed to get out, his eyes trying to focus. "Someone came in my window."

I glanced at the tinted window a little to the left of the makeup table. It was shut, but it only had a simple latch that could be jimmied as easily as the door, and it would have been easy enough to close it from the outside once the killer went back out.

"The killer must have drugged the orange juice first then slipped out and waited for him to drink it before coming back in again," I said.

"Couldn't have been you," Tweedledum said, finally getting out of my personal space. "No way you could have made it through that window."

I glowered at him. Back in my time, I could have taken him down with a single roundhouse kick. I could probably still do it, although I'd probably put my back out of joint in the process. The thing that really hurt was that he spoke the truth. I couldn't make it through that window anymore. It was about eight feet off the ground. Our killer was reasonably fit.

"Did you see who did this to you, Mr. Armstrong?" Tweedledee asked.

"No," he replied, shaking his head in an exaggerated way from side to side. He didn't have much control of his motor faculties. "A guy. Mask. Tied me up then put that bomb on the door. When someone came and knocked, I kicked that script at the door to warn them. Couldn't speak loud enough."

I noticed for the first time a script on the floor near the door, partially shredded from the explosion.

"Did the killer say anything?" the bodyguard asked.

"No. Wait, yes. Um, he said something like … 'Two birds with one stone.'"

I gulped. So, he really was gunning for me.

The police finally showed up, and everyone was cleared out. The set's physician whisked Cliff Armstrong away, and the police kept everyone who had come to the trailer for questioning. As they took us away, we passed by the back of the trailer. One of Cheerville's finest was already investigating the window. I didn't see anything except a scuff mark on the wall of the trailer, probably from a shoe. The window faced the back of a long semi-trailer truck that blocked it from view of the rest of the street and created a nice private little alley for the killer to sneak in the back way. Security was terrible on this picture.

Deliberately terrible?

After some dreary questioning in the security trailer, where I had to repeat my story several times,

Police Chief Arnold Grimal showed up. He gave me a sour look, hurried off to consult with his officers, then came back to see me several minutes later. He shut the door behind him so we could talk privately.

"Why do you always get yourself in the thick of it?" he grumbled.

"Yes, I'm fine. Thank you for asking."

Actually, my leg and elbow still hurt from hitting the ground, but I wasn't about to tell him that.

"Did your policeman notice that scuff mark by the window?" I asked.

"Of course! My officers are the best in the county."

I almost laughed at that, even though I didn't really feel in the laughing mood. "What did you find?" I asked, suppressing a smile.

"Forensics are checking on it now. Same with the bomb. They're dusting for prints as well."

"They won't find any. This fellow is too methodical for that, although at the same time, he makes odd slips. He could have killed Cliff Armstrong when he had the chance but instead went after me with a poorly designed bomb. By the way, I asked you to do a background check on Lars Mollan and find out the terms of the settlement he made with Cliff Armstrong. What did you discover?"

"That was barely an hour ago!" his voice came out in an adolescent whine more suitable for my grandson, Martin. That reminded me, I still needed to get them off the set somehow.

"And?"

"No criminal record in this state or California, which is the state where he resides. We haven't had time to find out the terms of the settlement."

"Fair enough. How's Cliff Armstrong?"

"Still doped. We took a blood sample, and we're having the orange juice checked, but we're pretty sure it's Rohypnol. It's easy enough to get on the Internet."

"Will he be all right?"

"Yeah. He didn't take much. He'll be fine in a few hours."

And he was fine in a few hours. By then Grimal had laid down the law. If Vance Randolph wanted to keep shooting his picture in Grimal's jurisdiction, he had to put in a lot of extra security measures. Any scene that Cliff Armstrong was in had to be sealed off with policemen and security. Only the cast and crew who were absolutely essential could get past the cordon. Also, two police officers would accompany the movie star everywhere.

I had to say I was impressed. Grimal had developed a bit of a backbone and stood up to these Hollywood types.

About time.

I had to go through makeup again (my brush with that bomb had ruined it), and when I passed through the police cordon, Vance Randolph himself was there to clear me and everyone else on the list.

Even so, I was thoroughly searched. The police didn't know my special status, and I didn't tell them. Better if they treated me no differently than anyone else.

The men were searched even more thoroughly than the women, and a police officer fired each musket in the air to make sure it was unloaded. The bayonets and swords were taken away. Vance Randolph complained that "reduced the historical veracity of the scene," but Grimal overruled him.

As I made it past the cordon, Harvey weaved his way through the crowd—and I do mean weaved—and took me by the elbow, more for his own support than any gentlemanly upbringing on his part.

"Mr. Great Movie Star wants to see you."

My mouth went dry. "Cliff Armstrong wants to see me?" Despite all that had happened, I was still somewhat starstruck.

He led me to a trailer. It wasn't the star's own

trailer since that was still a crime scene but a slightly smaller one that he had no doubt commandeered from one of his costars. Two police officers flanked the entrance.

Harvey introduced me. They looked at my ID and knocked on the door.

I was shown in and into the presence of a screen legend.

ELEVEN

Cliff Armstrong slumped in an easy chair, looking anything but a proud and confident action hero. The interior of the trailer was a scaled-down version of his own, minus the hot tub. So a four-star trailer rather than a five-star one. I wondered if that was what made him so obviously depressed.

He looked up when I came in and managed a faint smile.

"Ah, Old Widow Margaret Goode. Thanks for coming. Please sit down."

The thank-you took me aback. From what I'd heard and seen, he wasn't the thanking kind.

I sat in another easy chair near his. All my trepidation had gone. For some reason, sitting next to him in this dimly lit trailer made him seem more human, like I was visiting a rich and successful neighbor rather than a living legend.

"What's your name?" he asked. "I mean your real name."

"Barbara Gold. What's yours?"

He shrugged. "Actually, Cliff Armstrong is my real name. Well, Clifford, but only my mother called me that when she was still alive."

There was a pause. I shifted uneasily in my seat. Why was I here?

"I wanted to thank you for saving me," he said. The words seemed to take some effort.

"My pleasure. I think you would be a lot safer if we stopped production until we caught this murderer. You should go off to Tahiti or something."

He shook his head. "The show must go on. We were behind schedule when we got here, and we're even more behind schedule now."

"But why would someone want to kill you?"

That got the first spark of life I'd seen in him since I'd entered the trailer.

"They all want to kill me. They're all jealous of my success!"

"Can you think of anyone specific? Anyone you might have had a fight with?"

The movie star waved a dismissive hand. "Oh,

they all fight with me. That's how Gwendolyn got Bert killed."

"What?"

"She was getting all fussy about me having a little fun on the side. I don't see how it's any of her business. I've never gone out with her. I have enough paparazzi following me everywhere. If we got a thing going, I'd get all of her paparazzi too. But she doesn't see that. She's obsessed with me, and she kept nagging me in the church while we were waiting to do the scene." His voice took on a nasal whine. "'Why don't we go away somewhere? Nobody needs to know. You're too good for all those extras and script coaches.' Ugh, she's driving me nuts! I wanted to go out for the next take like I usually do, but the cameras started rolling before I could pull myself away. So Bert went instead."

"And got blown up in your place."

Cliff Armstrong shuddered. "That would have been me. Everyone knows I do all the takes with the special effects and stunts until the final one when the stuntman steps in. I'd perform that one myself too. I did a stint as a stuntman before I got discovered, but those damn insurance people don't let me. It's such a rip-off to the fans to have someone step in at the last moment and pretend to be me."

"Seems like Bert got the bad end of the deal, not the fans."

Cliff Armstrong nodded sadly. "Poor guy. Sure, he was little people, but he didn't deserve to die."

"He isn't the only little person to die," I said, unable to keep a slight edge from my voice.

"Oh yeah, that minuteman. Bob something."

"Randy Bowen."

"Who?"

"Randy Bowen was the minuteman actor who got killed by the boom mic."

"Oh."

He didn't seem too concerned. After a minute, he looked at me. He had not made much eye contact since I had entered the trailer. He seemed completely unlike the man who had first glad-handed me and Octavian in the crowd. Smaller. Far less confident.

"You know the fans are the only people who care about me?" he said.

"Oh, I'm sure that's not true." Actually, I had a feeling it was.

He shook his head sadly and let out a heaving sigh.

"Everyone thinks Hollywood is this glamorous, wonderful place to be, but it's a shark tank. Remember that shark tank I had to swim through to save the babies in *Sharkpocalypse II: Dying Really Bites?* Hollywood is worse than that. Everyone wanting something, everyone trying to rip you off, all those fake smiles …"

"Then why don't you quit?"

The movie star looked horrified. "Quit? Then I'd lose the fans. I'd lose everything!"

I seemed to recall reading that Cliff Armstrong had been an only child. He was not married and had no children of his own. I suspected both his parents were dead. Yes, this man really was alone.

He studied me for a moment. "You seem so nice. Why would you want to be a part of all this craziness?"

"I guess I was a bit starstruck," I admitted.

"Get out. It will corrupt you. This is the loneliest job in the world."

I almost blurted out something reassuring. I almost pointed out to him that he had millions of adoring fans, that he had throngs of beautiful women throwing themselves at him, that his face was known the world over.

But I bit my tongue. Because I realized that he was right. After a minute, he spoke.

"Sometimes I think Harvey has the right answer. Just drink yourself into oblivion. But I can't do that. Too pathetic. Can't take drugs either. Yeah,

I know nobody believes me in all those public service announcements, but I really am one hundred percent sober. Always have been. That's left me far too sane for this crazy business."

"So, what will you do?"

He slapped his knees and stood up. Suddenly he was Cliff Armstrong again—strong, confident, ready. The transformation took only a second, and it was complete. "What will *I* do? You mean what will *we* do! We have a movie to make! You and I are going to march out there and become General John T. Slaughter and Old Widow Margaret Goode, and we're going to do that so well we'll knock 'em out of their seats!"

I actually stood up and saluted. "Sir, yes, sir!"

Automatic reaction. I can't help it.

He shot me his winning grin and clapped his hands three times. "That's the spirit. Let's do it!"

And we did. It was the campfire scene. Everything was as it had been before, minus one minuteman, plus a boom mic operator with a bandage around his head and two cops standing just outside the circle of light. Even if they hadn't been in uniform, I could have told they were cops. They were the only people not looking at the scene.

"Got your—*hic*—lines memorized?" Harvey asked as we got there.

Cliff Armstrong swayed back and forth. "Yes —*hic*—Harvey. She—*hic*—does. She's a—*hic*—pro, unlike you."

"Bleep off you bleeping bleeper," Harvey said, storming off. Well, he tried to storm off. As it turned out, he stormed a good ten feet or so before he tripped over a power cable and nearly took a nose-dive. "BLEEP!" he shouted at the electrician who was setting up the cables. "Watch what you're bleeping doing!"

I rounded on the movie star. "You don't have to make fun of him like that. It's cruel."

I expected him to be defiant or to laugh me off, but instead he looked at me like a chastened schoolchild.

"Sorry," he mumbled. "Let's get to our marks."

So we went through the familiar scene once again. Cliff Armstrong sat in a camp chair in front of the fake campfire, surrounded by his men. The cameras were set close to the actors, cutting out the city and street that were just a few feet away from the patch of grass where the men stood and sat. I hovered to one side, ready to make my entrance.

"Remember—*hic*—act all flustered and out of breath," Harvey said from behind me, enveloping me in a cloud of vodka fumes. Despite his outburst, he had promptly gotten back to his post. "You just ran through the woods at night. You're scared and tired but ready to do your duty no matter what the personal risk."

Been there, done that.

"Roll 'em!" Vance Randolph called.

Harvey made a pushing motion with his hands. I rushed into the shot, acting panicked and out of breath. That was easy. I just had to bring up the memories of the first time I came under hostile fire.

"General Slaughter! General Slaughter!" I called out, rushing toward Cliff Armstrong.

One of the minutemen interceded. "Stop right there! Who are you?"

I acted meek, hunching over a little. "The Widow Margaret Goode, sir. I have important news for General Slaughter."

"She could be a spy," the minuteman said over his shoulder to the others.

"Nonsense," Cliff Armstrong said. "Look in her eyes. No deception lies hidden there. She's a tried and true American. I would bet my britches."

"Care to make a wager?" Pretty Boy asked.

"Ha! You'd lose, my good man, and would have to defeat the British in your long johns," Cliff Armstrong said as he stood up. He walked over to me and took my hands. "Sit down, old woman.

Here, take my seat. Someone get her some hot broth. The night is cold."

"Oh, thank you, good sir," I said, taking a steaming cup from one of the minutemen. I almost lost it when I looked inside. Instead of an actual cup of steaming broth, the cup was empty except for a little chunk of dry ice that sent up a cloud that looked like steam. Wouldn't the real thing be more realistic? I tilted it a little away from the camera so the audience wouldn't notice and pretended to take a sip.

Cliff Armstrong stood next to me, his fists on his hips. "So, good widow, what is this important news you have for me?"

"The evil British general is billeting in my poor humble cabin, sir." *Did people really talk like this back then?* "And I overheard him conspiring with his officers to hatch an evil plan. They intend to attack you on the Sabbath, sir, when your men are at church."

"Bah, I should have known! The British are a godless lot, unlike we great Americans."

I leaned in a little closer to my favorite movie star. There was a time, not more than twenty-four hours ago, when that would have made me feel giddy, but he had become human now. All too human. "They say they will strike half an hour after the church bells ring for service, to make sure that most of the minutemen are inside the church. Then one group of redcoats will attack the camp while it is lightly guarded, and the rest will surround the church and burn it to the ground!"

"The beasts!" Cliff Armstrong thundered.

"Watch out!" a woman's voice cried from off camera.

"Cut!" Vance Randolph called, but his voice was barely heard as a chorus of shouts went up from the crew. Cliff Armstrong ducked and scampered behind the minutemen. I squinted, trying to see through the harsh glare of the lights. There was the sound of a scuffle and more shouting.

I stepped forward, out past the lights, where I could see. It took a moment for my eyes to adjust. When they did, I saw the electrician who had tripped up Harvey struggling with a couple of teamsters right next to one of the main power cables, the same one Harvey had tripped over. The cops rushed for him.

"I didn't do anything!" the electrician cried as the cops yanked him away from the teamsters. "I was only checking the connection for the artificial fire light."

The script coach, Mary Ellworth, pointed an accusing finger. "He was trying to splice in that portable generator. That would have overcharged the artificial fire and made it blow up in Cliff Armstrong's face."

There was, indeed, a portable generator nearby. A cord ran from it to just behind where the electrician stood. He looked to where Mary was pointing, and his eyes went wide.

"I didn't put that there. I swear!"

"He looks the same size as the guy who hit Clyde over the head," Mary said. "I didn't get to see his face because of the hood, but he's got the same body dimensions."

"Looks like we got our man," the police said. "If he's an electrician, he could have set up those explosions easy."

Cliff Armstrong stepped away from the set and peered at the struggling man.

"William? I should have known. You're still sore that I stole that girl from you a couple pictures back. But seriously, man, you'd kill me over a bit of skirt? She wasn't even that good in bed."

I frowned at the movie star.

William put on an innocent face. "I swear it wasn't me. Wait, it couldn't have been me. I was setting up for the river scene when the explosions went off in the town square. I was miles away!"

"Can you prove it?" one of the cops asked.

"I can disprove it," Mary said. "I saw you at the

town square. Mr. Randolph, get the master schedule, and you'll see I'm right."

"What's that?" I asked Cliff Armstrong.

"It shows where everyone was working at a certain time," he replied. "One of his assistants has to sign off on everything. It lists everything so that everyone gets the right pay. Union regulations."

The director climbed down from his high chair and summoned over an assistant toting a thick ledger. They looked at it together for a minute. A tense silence fell on the set as everyone waited.

Then the director looked up. "It wasn't him. He was supposed to be on the town square, but the setup for the river scene was having some trouble, and he got sent over there at the last minute."

"But I saw him at the town square!" Mary protested.

Vance Randolph nodded. "Yes, you did, but he left half an hour before Bert got killed. No way he could have been the one."

I slumped. It looked like this case hadn't been solved after all. One of the cops spoke up.

"We'll need to take him in for questioning anyway. Let's see that ledger, and find some of the river-scene crew who can vouch for him."

"You'll find plenty," William said, looking more confident now.

Mary hung her head. "I'm sorry. I could have sworn you were going to hook that power cable up."

"Yeah, what about that?" I asked.

William shrugged. "I have no idea."

And that clinched it. Anyone who is guilty will think of an alibi in a nanosecond. They'll blurt out an answer to any question you may have. William really was innocent.

"Could the power cable have been for any other use?" I asked.

William shook his head. "No. It looks like it was going to be hooked up to the artificial fire just like Mary said."

"Who else was near this cable?"

"Well, me," Mary admitted.

"Yeah, but you didn't touch it," another man wearing a worker's uniform said. "I could see your every move."

Mary gave him an uncertain smile.

"Did you see what I did, Gary?" William asked.

"No, sorry. I was too focused on the shoot. I didn't notice you until Mary pointed you out."

William shrugged. "It's okay. The guys at the river shoot will bear me out."

A few calls were made, and half a dozen people from the crew were called in. No work got done while we waited. Everyone was too focused on unraveling the truth about William's story.

It turned out he was telling the truth. All of the crew from the river shoot swore he had been with them. Then a second unit cameraman appeared with some rough footage of the river he had taken to decide on framing and lighting of the shots. We put it through a computer by Vance Randolph's seat, and we saw, in the distance but clearly enough, William at one edge of the frame, working on some wiring. The time stamp was just a few minutes after the attack on Cliff Armstrong.

"No way he could have made it to the river on time," one of the cops said. He sounded as disappointed as I felt.

Mary put words to what we were all thinking. "So, he's innocent? That means this nightmare will continue!"

TWELVE

I got home exhausted, both from the stress of nearly being killed and the tension of being in a movie. I'd been on the set for twelve hours. All I wanted to do was take a long hot bath to ease my aching joints, the bruises I got from my dive into the concrete, and a throbbing headache that had come out of nowhere. Stress headaches weren't my thing —if they had been, I never could have worked for the CIA—but I was way out of my comfort zone on this case. After that hot bath, maybe I should put something stronger in my tea to help me rest. Harvey might be onto something.

But first I had to see what Police Chief Grimal had learned, if anything. It was late, but I figured with this fire-breathing dragon of a case on his back, he would still be at work.

I put a call in to Grimal's office. It took some time to get him on the line.

Yes, I still call it "a line." There used to be a line when I was growing up. And, yes, I do use a cell phone, thank you very much.

"So, what have you found?" I demanded. Not asked, demanded. Anytime I ask something of Grimal I end up having to demand it anyway. Best just to cut to the chase.

"A few things," Grimal grumbled, obviously not wanting to speak with me. His mouth sounded like it was half-full of something. I suspected I had interrupted his Chinese takeaway.

"Such as?"

"The switchboard, the one used to control the explosions on the town square. At first we couldn't figure out how the murderer used it. It's encased in a steel box that was shut and locked. Standard procedure when the technician walks away to avoid accidents. Plus the technician disconnected it from the generator. As you know, the head technician and several other witnesses checked it as soon as the stuntman was killed. The box was still locked and unplugged. We traced all the power lines. That took some time. It's like ground control at Cape Canaveral at that place. Anyway, we found a splice in the line going to the explosive charges. The extra line led to a storage trailer that had a window with a good view of the square. The trailer was unlocked. Unfortunately, there was nothing at the end of that electrical line. But it's easy to figure out what was there—a second control panel. The murderer was then able to take over the detonation of the charges."

"Oh dear. So, their safety measures are proof against accidents but not against murder."

"Yup." Actually, that came out more as "Glup." I pictured Grimal slurping down some sweet and sour chicken.

"So, our murderer has some technical savvy and access to what I suppose is an expensive and not terribly common bit of hardware."

"We're working on the theory that he's associated with the film."

I gave my best teenage eye roll. My grandson is a good teacher, and Grimal is good inspiration.

"Yes, I think that's probably correct," I said, keeping my voice level. "What did you find out about the insurance?"

"Both the film and Cliff Armstrong are insured to the hilt. But here's the catch. The insurance company they're using is notorious for dumping production companies that prove a liability. There have been a couple of cases where pictures have run into trouble and had to claim insurance from these guys. The company lives up to its contract and pays the claim, but that's it. They'll never cover that production company again, and they spread the word that no other company should either. That's the kiss of death for the producers."

"Ouch. So that's why the Hollywood bigwigs are so desperate to keep this picture going. And Cliff Armstrong?"

"Ah, he's worth millions if he dies."

"Who's the beneficiary?"

"That's privileged information. I'd need a court order to find that out."

"Who took out the policy?"

"The studio."

"Then we know the beneficiary."

"We do? Oh yeah, we do."

More eye rolling.

"Did you find out anything about the terms of the settlement Lars Mollan made with Cliff Armstrong after that fight?"

"Once again, privileged information. I have a buddy in the LAPD. We went to the police academy together. He bent a few ears and found out there was a cash settlement and a promise of employment. I don't know the details. Basically, in exchange for not causing trouble for Cliff Armstrong's career, Lars Mollan got job security."

"And a prime opportunity to get in close to the man who humiliated him and plot his murder."

"Nope."

"Pardon me?" I wasn't sure if he had said that or had simply been slurping down more Chinese takeaway.

"We've been keeping an eye on the guy ever since we found out about him. He was in the CGI lab for more than an hour before Cliff Armstrong got drugged and stayed there the whole time the star was tied up and the bomb was set."

"Oh."

"Yeah." Grimal's voice shared my disappointment. It had been a good lead, the obvious lead, but it didn't look like it was going anywhere.

I hadn't crossed him off the list of suspects entirely yet. There was still the possibility of a conspiracy of which Mollan was a part.

"Keep an eye on him," I ordered. There was a knock at my door. "Anything else?"

"Hmm?" he said around a mouthful of food. He swallowed. It sounded loud and more than a little disgusting in my ear. "Um, no. We have every man on it. The murderer would have a hell of a time reaching him now."

"Don't underestimate the guy or girl or group. Yes, it might be a group. Keep at it. Oh, and the footprint on Cliff Armstrong's trailer?"

"Sneaker. Unknown brand. Size ten and a half."

That meant a man.

I hung up. The knocking at my front door repeated.

"One minute!" I called in a singsong voice. I hurried to my bedroom and pulled my nine-millimeter automatic from my bedside table. After the suspect had tried to bushwhack me and then tried to blow me up, I wasn't taking any more chances.

I went to the door, stood to one side, and put my finger over the spyhole.

This is a common precaution. Any observant person will notice the light in the spyhole get blocked out from the inside, showing that someone is at home and looking through the door. It's a simple thing to put a bullet through the area and hit the person on the other side. No, the average American front door isn't bulletproof. It isn't even kick-proof. So I put my finger over the spyhole in case there's a shooter on the other side. The worst that will happen is I lose my finger instead of my head.

No shots came, so I took a look through the hole.

And got quite a shock.

It was Liz. I'd met Liz at a nudist colony …

Wait. Allow me to clarify. I was investigating a murder at a nudist colony when I got some much-needed help from one of its members.

Liz was a bit of a cipher. Forties, fit, perceptive, she figured out that a hit-and-run death of one of the nudist colony members had been murder and was well on her way to solving it even without me. She claimed to have been a forward observer in the United States Army during a couple of foreign wars. A forward observer goes to the very front of the line, or even a little beyond, in order to call back enemy positions so the artillery can home in on them.

I say "claims" because, while being a forward observer required intelligence and courage, Liz seemed to have a skill set way beyond that. I suspected she had done some other duty, one that had taken her *behind* enemy lines.

Not that she was going to tell me.

I opened up.

"Good evening," I said. "I'm not going to ask how you found my address."

"Hello," Liz said with a smile. "And I'm not going to insult your intelligence by telling you. I'm sure you can figure that out yourself."

"Tea? I was just about to make myself some."

"Thank you."

She sat down on the sofa, and Dandelion immediately leaped onto her and curled up in her lap. Dandelion is normally a skittish little ball of fur, so I took that for a good sign. She didn't do that with the hired assassin that broke into my house a while back, that's for sure.

"So, how's everything at the nudist colony?" I asked as I fussed about the kitchen.

"Good. Everyone is gradually healing after what happened. The finances are a mess. We're going to pool together to buy it and run it as a cooperative."

"Oh, that's good news."

I wasn't just being polite. They seemed like a good group of people. For the most part. A bit odd in their lifestyle choices, but I didn't judge.

For a time, neither of us spoke. I kept my ears perked. For some reason I thought she might snoop around the place while I was in the kitchen. I trusted her, but I didn't know what she was all about. She could say the same about me.

As the kettle started to whistle, I used the sound to mask my movements, went to the doorway that opened onto the living room, and peeked out.

Liz was still sitting on the sofa, petting my cat. She hadn't done anything. I felt oddly disappointed.

I poured the water into the teapot, put it on a tray with two cups and some cookies, and returned to the living room.

"How did you hurt yourself?" Liz asked, indicating the lacerations on my arm.

"Dove away from a booby-trapped door."

I might as well be honest, shouldn't I?

Liz chuckled. "You'll never retire, will you?"

She didn't know exactly what I had retired from, but she could narrow it down pretty well.

"I don't suppose you will either. Milk and sugar?"

"Please. One lump."

"No sugar for me," I said. "I got enough lumps today as it is."

"I saw you all dressed up for the movie," Liz said.

"And so you knew I had infiltrated the set in order to find the person who's trying to kill Cliff Armstrong."

As interesting as this conversation was, I was very weary and wanted to get through it as quickly as possible.

Liz nodded and took a sip. "How can I help?" she asked.

I was hoping she was going to ask that.

"Are you an officer of the law?" I asked.

"Isn't citizen's arrest good enough for you?"

That wasn't exactly an answer to my question. I let it slide.

"Can you get onto the set?" I asked.

Liz shrugged. "With the new security measures, it will be tough. I was thinking I could go as your assistant."

"I only have a very small role."

"You have a speaking role with Cliff Armstrong. That doesn't sound small to me."

I set my teacup down. "How on Earth did you hear that?"

"I had my hair done today. Do you like it? Everyone at the hairdresser's is abuzz with who got what role. Your name came up. Some people would kill for a chance to act beside him."

"Oh, they want to kill all right but not for that reason."

I should have known talk would get around. Nothing stays private in a little town like Cheerville for long. I could only thank the Great CIA Director in the Sky that no one had learned I had a membership to a nudist colony.

Well, my grandson Martin had. I had to tell him a half-truth about being a secret sheriff's deputy. I'd been basking in admiration ever since.

"I may have a speaking role, but it's really quite

small. I've seen quite a hierarchy on this set. I suppose it's normal in Hollywood. The stars are waited on hand and foot, and everyone else just muddles through by themselves. It's caviar and hot tubs or tuna fish sandwiches and plastic chairs. There's no way I could demand to have an assistant. They'd laugh in my face."

Liz thought for a moment then snapped her fingers. "I know. I can be your nurse!"

"My nurse?"

"You have a chronic condition and need medical supervision."

"Wouldn't they fire me?"

"We could threaten to sue. It's called ableism."

"Ableism?"

"Discrimination against the disabled."

"Young lady, I am not disabled!"

Liz closed her eyes and smiled. "That's why I like hanging out with you. You call me young."

I almost laughed but then remembered when I was in my forties, way back when big hair was in and the Sony Walkman was the height of consumer technology, how I thought I was getting old too.

"But how can you fake being a nurse? Wait, are you a nurse?"

"I got Advanced First Aid in the Army. I can talk the talk."

"But what about the uniform and ID?"

"I can take care of that."

Of course you can.

"Just who are you anyway?" I demanded.

She looked at me. "A friend who wants to help you stop a murderer. Isn't that good enough?"

I smiled. "Yes, dear. Yes, it is."

We set to work.

THIRTEEN

The next day, I arrived at the movie set with my very own fake nurse.

Liz had done herself up in a nurse's uniform, complete with an ID from the Nurses' Union and a medical letter saying that I had a chronic heart condition. Because of the shock from the bomb, I was in danger of heart failure and needed to be monitored. She had even brought along a defibrillator.

I was impressed by how quickly she got all that stuff together. I bet it was even all legit. It only confirmed my suspicions that she was far more than a clever veteran who liked to play nude volleyball in her off hours.

We were, of course, stopped at the perimeter. Grimal's police officers gave us trouble until Vance

Randolph, who was monitoring who came in for the day, intervened.

"The old woman is all right," he told them. "She wasn't even in the cast when Bert got killed. And she chased after the guy when Randy was murdered."

They let "the old woman" and her nurse in. The director inquired about my health, no doubt more out of fear of losing another Old Widow Margaret Goode than any solicitude about my safety. Liz reassured him.

"As long as she doesn't have any sudden shocks, she should be fine. Also, when she's not on camera, it would be best for her to get away from the set. All the lights and hustle and bustle will stress her."

Vance Randolph quickly agreed to that and went back to checking on the others coming through the police cordon.

Clever girl. She had just given us the right to snoop.

And snoop we did. After checking in with a hungover Harvey to discover that my next scene, a crowd scene in the town square, wasn't scheduled to shoot for another two hours, we took the opportunity to have a look around.

One disadvantage was that our cover story limited us to sticking together. This meant we could only cover half the ground we should have been able to, and there was a lot of ground to cover. The sets and trailers sprawled through the center of Cheerville like a town within a town. I couldn't even begin to count the places where the murderer might choose to strike next.

We started with the electrical facilities. The first murder attempt, the one that caught poor Bert in the crossfire, had been done with considerable technological savvy. And the incident last night had raised my suspicions. Had that cable connected to the generator been ready to splice into the artificial fire like the script coach had suspected? It had been proven that William wasn't the murderer (unless he was part of a conspiracy), but that didn't mean the cable had just been lying there all sweet and innocent. Movie sets seemed chaotic on the surface, but people knew their work and did it. A potentially hazardous cable wouldn't be sitting like a venomous snake right next to a set.

So we wandered around, peeking into vans equipped with expensive computers and tables covered in electronic equipment I couldn't even name let alone discern the use of. Everything seemed in order, at least as far as we could tell. We saw no suspicious activity. On the other hand, so much of what they were doing was so unclear to us that it was hard to know what was suspicious and what was normal.

It was a frustrating search, that is, until we came across two technicians rushing into and out of a trailer, carting out small wheeled platforms that had racks of metal tubes on them. They looked for all the world like mortar tubes from the Army, except each platform had about fifty of them. Electrical connections were attached to each one, and another wheeled platform carried an electronic control panel. A truck backed up, and a teamster began loading the racks of tubes into the back.

When one of the technicians came out again and turned to say something to the teamster, I saw the back of his shirt was emblazoned with the words "Big Bang Fireworks Company: Creating a Universe of Color."

After giving the teamster some instructions on how to load everything, he went back into the trailer, only to emerge with his colleague a minute later. Both carried large boxes labeled "Explosive: Handle with Care."

We had just turned to continue our search when we heard the technician say, "Well, they got to be somewhere. Look again!"

Liz and I exchanged glances. The two men disappeared into the trailer. There was some discussion inside. The teamster was out of sight, moving things around in the back of the truck, so we crept closer to the trailer.

"There are supposed to be eight crates," we heard the technician say. "There's only seven. Where's the other one?"

"How the hell am I supposed to know? Maybe they never delivered it."

"We'll deal with this later. We're late enough as it is. The shoot only needs four crates anyway. Let's just hope they don't ask for another take."

We lingered for a minute but heard nothing else. Then one of the men emerged and spotted us.

"Can I help you?" he challenged.

"Oh, no," I said in my sweet grandma voice. "I'm just resting here out of the sun. It's ever so tiring to be in a movie."

He softened at that.

"All right," he said. "But you're going to have to rest somewhere else. This is where we keep the fireworks, and only qualified personnel can be around here."

I was tempted to ask if having blown up bridges in Latin America made me "qualified personnel." Instead I smiled, and we moved on.

"Some explosives are missing. That's bad news," Liz said in a low voice as we moved off.

She didn't say "fireworks," so she knew the potential of this situation. Fireworks are, of course, explosives. They can be cut open and the explosive chemical compounds removed and put together to make a crude bomb. All it would need was a fuse and a source of fire. The fireworks themselves each had a fuse, and they could be ignited in any number of ways—such as an electric charge or even a simple cigarette lighter.

Someone had just stolen bomb-making supplies. I put a call in to Grimal but found he was out. I instructed the officer who answered my call to relay my message immediately.

I'd warn the security here myself.

It was now time for my next scene, and I figured I could go there and tell the first security officer I saw. Harvey had told me we were shooting next to Cheerville's old one-room schoolhouse. No one seemed to mind that it dated to almost a century after the American Revolution. I suppose the average moviegoer isn't an expert on historical one-room-schoolhouse architecture.

The schoolhouse is a small stone building next to the town square. The front door opens onto the green. Cameras had been set up in a half circle facing the door. As we gathered, Vance Randolph shouted to us through his megaphone from atop his little perch.

"Okay, this is one of the finale scenes. The British have been defeated, and America has won her freedom. This is a big triumphant scene where school has reopened. The kids are running out the front door into the arms of their loving parents. General Slaughter has just been teaching them a lesson about freedom and will stride out in front of them. In the background, we're going to have a bunch of fireworks going off. Don't be distracted by all those. Just look at your children and lift them up in your arms when they get to you."

My heart turned to ice. Fireworks. I turned to Liz and saw her thinking the same thing.

Frantically I looked around and spotted my son Frederick standing on the other side of the crowd, nearly a hundred yards away to my left. My grandson Martin was not with him.

Of course he wasn't. He was in the schoolhouse with Cliff Armstrong, the walking target.

And they'd be running straight into a fusillade of fireworks.

But wait, the fireworks were set up *behind* the schoolhouse. They couldn't fire at the entrance.

Unless the killer had already cut them open and made a bomb with them.

I looked desperately at the ground between us and the schoolhouse, wondering if the killer had made some sort of crude landmine. I didn't see any disturbed earth and soon discarded the idea. Planting it would have been too conspicuous.

Unless ...

"Liz, we have to find that—"

Vance Randolph's booming voice cut me off. "Okay, positions, everybody."

Liz caught my meaning. Both of us scanned the crowd.

"Quiet on the set! Ready ..."

"There!" I said, pointing to a spot in the crowd about fifty yards to the right of us.

A man in the shabby clothing of a poor peddler stood behind an apple cart. The cart was the only thing in view that could hide a bomb, and it was right in front of the crowd. There was nothing between it and the front door of the schoolhouse except a few yards of open space.

Then I realized it wasn't a bomb at all but one of those firework launchers hidden under the cart. A thin sheet hung around the sides. The peddler was just lifting it up to reveal the launcher clamped to the bottom of the cart, its tubes pointing not up but toward the schoolhouse.

And something about the man looked familiar.

He had a shapeless felt hat slouched low over his face, so it took a second, but then I recognized him.

Gary, the other electrician from the shoot last night. He had been on the scene, close to the cable.

"Stop Gary! He's the murderer!" I shouted.

My voice got drowned out by Vance Randolph's megaphone.

"Roll 'em!"

The door to the schoolhouse opened, and Cliff Armstrong strode out. Just behind him I could see a crowd of children.

Martin was right in front.

Liz was already running for the apple cart. I ran after her, with the horrible knowledge that my sore ankles and knees would not get me there in time.

As if in slow motion, I saw fireworks rise up from behind the schoolhouse, sending fiery red, white, and blue trails up into the sky and end by bursting into giant rosettes. Gary bent down behind the apple cart, his hand turning something. He looked back at Cliff Armstrong and the children running out of the school and closed one eye.

As if he was aiming.

That's when Liz hit him.

More accurately, she hit the cart, a full-on body slam that sent the cart tipping over backward. Apples cascaded off, making Gary stagger back.

The next moment there was a blinding flash as dozens of fireworks shot out from the side of the cart and roared into the air.

My eardrums throbbed, and my eyes stung. I blinked and brought up my hands, unable to see for the dazzling light.

But I kept running.

Boom. Boom. Boom.

One by one the fireworks went off. Trailers of flame arched over us, blotting out the sky with a multicolored canopy of lights.

It would have been beautiful if it hadn't almost burnt my grandson into cinders.

I kept running, the screams of the parting crowd jabbing my ringing ears.

I came to the apple cart to find Liz curled up in a ball next to it. She didn't look hurt, but lying right next to the launch point, she must have been deafened, blinded, and a bit singed. She wouldn't be any help for the moment.

And I needed help. Through the haze of acrid smoke, I saw Gary staggering away. He had one hand clutched to his face, and I suspected he wasn't much better off than Liz. The rest of the crowd was running away, too, and I feared that he'd get lost in the muddle.

I went after him.

As I said, I am not terribly fast on my feet anymore, but Gary was stumbling and seemed dazed, and I gained ground on him. Obviously, he had been standing too close to the launch of the fireworks. Hadn't he thought of this when he set up his attack? Was I dealing with a madman?

Mad or no, he had twenty inches and at least a hundred pounds on me, so I decided to get this over with quickly. Running up behind him, I kicked him with the flat of my foot right behind the knee.

He never heard me coming. With that blast of fireworks right next to him, I could have been Hannibal chasing him with a herd of elephants and he wouldn't have heard me.

My kick landed perfectly, and down he went. My next kick was to the kneecap to keep him there.

He squalled. I circled around him so I could give him a kick to the head. Not terribly ladylike, I know, but he had tried to hurt my family.

Just as I pulled my leg back to clock him in the temple and knock him out, he pulled a box cutter from his pocket, pushed on the release, and deployed a nasty razor-sharp blade.

I backpedaled. There was a time when I would have kicked it right out of his hand, breaking his fingers in the process. That time had long passed.

He staggered to his feet, favoring his uninjured

leg. His face was burned, one eye shut, the other bugging out wildly.

He lunged with the box cutter. I just managed to dodge out of the way, circling to his weak side.

Then I had to back off again, and he swung his long arm, the razor blade gleaming in the light as it missed me by an inch.

I backed off again. His one eye, bloodshot and livid, fixed me with a hungry glare.

And I knew I was too slow to get out of this one.

FOURTEEN

The box cutter swung at me. I ducked, always a good tactic when you're a short person fighting a tall one, and punched him in the ribs.

That barely elicited a grunt from my opponent, and I pulled back again, knuckles smarting.

"Huzzah!" someone shouted. A golden blur flew through the air, and an eighteenth-century boot smacked Gary in the jaw. The madman pirouetted, falling to the ground.

Cliff Armstrong stood over him.

"Unhand that fair maiden, you varlet!"

"Wrong century," I said as the movie star of my dreams put one knee on Gary's chest and started punching him with a meaty fist.

Gary struggled but could not get free. His hands

flopped over the grass then found the box cutter. His fingers wrapped around it, muscles tense, ready to gut Cliff Armstrong.

So I kicked Gary in the head. Like I said, not very ladylike, but this isn't the Girl Scouts.

I got him right in the temple, and he went out like a light.

Cliff Armstrong looked up at me in wonder.

"Huzzah?" I asked, arching one eyebrow.

He shrugged. "It sounded like the proper thing to say." He stood. "And to you, fair lady, I say thank you." He took me in his arms and gave me a kiss on the cheek.

Things got a bit hazy after that. I was floating on a dreamy cloud of adrenaline and fulfilled fantasy. I remember a big crowd gathering. The police who were supposed to be watching over Cliff Armstrong (who still had his beefy, perfectly proportioned arm around my shoulder, helping to keep me from keeling over while simultaneously giving me a reason to) finally showed up and cuffed Gary.

"Why did you do it?" Vance Randolph asked. Gary had come to, although he still looked a bit groggy, thanks to the pummeling we had given him.

Gary only sneered.

The police read him his rights. The director and

several others crowding around pestered him with questions, but Gary looked like he was going to use his right to remain silent.

I looked up at Cliff Armstrong and, I must admit, snuggled a bit closer to him.

"Why would he want to kill you?" I asked.

The movie star slowly shook his head. "I have no idea. I don't think I've ever spoken to him."

Liz staggered up to me. She looked as dazed as I felt.

"Are you okay?" I asked.

"My ears are ringing so much I didn't hear what you just said. If you're asking if I'm okay, the answer is yes. Well, I will be after a long nap and a couple of beers. You?"

I nodded and gave her a thumbs-up.

My son and grandson pushed through the crowd. That snapped me out of my dreamy fog of movie-star kisses.

Martin gave me a big hug. "You're a hero, Grandma!" He lowered his voice. "You were being a deputy, just like last time, right?"

I smiled down at him, basking in the approval. Nodding, I put my finger to my lips. It was our little secret. He beamed at me. There had been a time, not too long ago, when he had been too cool to hang out with his grandmother. Luckily, we had gotten over that hurdle.

"She sure is!" Cliff Armstrong boomed. "I think we need to rewrite the script to give a bigger role to Old Widow Margaret Goode."

More scenes with Cliff Armstrong? Be still my heart!

"We don't have the time to rewrite the script," Vance Randolph objected. "We're behind enough as it is."

Cliff Armstrong grew red. "You ungrateful idiot. She just saved me and every kid on this cast, not to mention your lousy picture! You're going to deny her a few extra lines just because of some schedule? I'm so sick of selfish amateurs like you."

Amateur? Vance Randolph had won an Oscar for Best Director and three for Best Picture.

I put a hand on Cliff Armstrong's chest. It felt like I was touching a Greek statue. A Greek statue that felt warm and had an intoxicating masculine scent. "You need to be more patient with your coworkers. You're all on the same team."

Cliff Armstrong looked chastened. He turned back to the director.

"Sorry I snapped at you, Mr. Randolph."

The director's jaw dropped in shock. Actually, everyone's did.

"Well … I … um, I guess we could put her in some of the lobby cards and promotional material," Vance Randolph sputtered.

Cliff Armstrong flashed a grin. "That would be great. Thanks!"

That got another shocked reaction from the cast and crew.

Mary Ellworth pushed through the crowd, an open script in her hand.

"Actually, there are a few spots where we could slip her in. Look here."

She pushed the script forward. Cliff Armstrong moved closer, craning his neck to look at the lines.

And something he had said in his trailer shot through my mind. Something his costar Gwendolyn Parker had told him. *"You're too good for all those extras and script coaches."*

I leaped forward, bringing up my hand to slap the script away.

A streak of hot pain lashed the palm of my hand. As the script flew to one side, we could all see the knife Mary held hidden underneath.

"Heartbreaker!" Mary shouted, lunging for Cliff Armstrong.

I got her just in time. Ignoring the pain in my palm, I gripped her wrist and used my other hand to bend her knife hand backward. If you do it right, you don't need to be very strong, and I had trained with this move for years. Mary let out a cry of pain, and the knife fell to the ground. A couple of the extras grabbed her arms. One of the film security personnel took over and cuffed her while Liz fetched her medical kit.

"Are you all right? What happened?" my son, Frederick, asked. Blocked by the crowd, they hadn't seen what had happened. Good. The less they knew about my abilities the better. I had hidden my career from him all his life. I wasn't about to reveal myself now.

"The script coach cut me while trying to get at Cliff Armstrong," I said. The cut was bleeding a lot but didn't look too deep. Hurt like the dickens, though. I turned to Mary Ellworth. "You had an affair with him, didn't you?"

"An affair? Ha! It barely lasted a week before I got tossed aside for someone from catering. Do you even remember what movie that was?"

Cliff Armstrong looked embarrassed. "Uh, no. But it was a while ago, wasn't it? Why are you still angry at me?"

"I'm not the one who's really angry. I said yes and had fun. Sure, the rejection hurt, but it hurt Gary a lot more."

"You were dating Gary?" the movie star asked, looking confused. "You told me you were single."

Mary hung her head. "I lied. I cheated on him because I was so flattered you were flirting with me. He went insane with rage when he found out. He never blamed me. He insisted that you seduced me or forced me. No matter how many times I told him it was my fault, he wouldn't listen. I ended up breaking up with him because he couldn't let it go, and that just made him worse."

"So you helped him try to kill me?"

Mary shook her head. "No. Gary never told me he was going to try to kill you. I figured it out, though, when he tried to blow you up."

Cliff Armstrong looked shocked. "Why didn't you go to the cops? He could have killed me!"

"And he did kill Bert," I reminded him.

"Oh yeah."

I hoped Frederick had pulled my grandson out of earshot. I didn't want him hearing this conversation. It was bad enough that I knew my movie-star hero had feet of clay. I didn't want poor little Martin to find that out too.

Mary hung her head. "I couldn't. I just couldn't. I love him, even if he is crazy. I tried to reason with him and make him promise not to go through with it again. But he got even crazier than before. He actually blamed you for Bert's death!"

"You should have gone to the police," Vance Randolph said.

"I couldn't," Mary whispered. "He'd have been locked up in a lunatic asylum, and Mr. Great Movie Star here would have been free to break up more relationships. Plus I was … afraid of him. I thought he might hurt me." She turned to me. "When he dropped the boom mic, I pointed him out to you, remember?"

"That's not enough," I said. "You figured he would get away from me, and you only said something because you were standing so close you obviously saw him knock out the boom-mic operator. You could have named him. Take responsibility, Mary. You are an accessory to murder. You even let me open that trailer door and nearly get blown up by a pipe bomb. Good thing Gary had been trained in safety so thoroughly that he didn't know how to make an effective bomb, otherwise I would have been killed and Cliff Armstrong along with me."

"I didn't know he was going to do that. I swear," Mary pleaded.

"Forgive me if I don't believe you. Besides, I would have never been in danger if you had told the police in the first place. And then you tried to finger William when Gary made his next attempt. The police were right there, and you could have told them, but you let Gary go once again then let him try a final time. How many people would he have killed or maimed with those fireworks? How many children?"

Mary didn't reply.

I shook my head in disgust. I had met all kinds of people in my career in the CIA—drug lords and mercenaries and tin-pot dictators—but no one had earned more of my contempt than this weak woman who let her crazy ex-boyfriend do her killing for her.

"Take her away," I sighed, turning my back and pushing through the crowd. I wanted to see my family.

A WEEK LATER, everything had settled down. At the preliminary hearing, Gary was judged to be criminally insane and would be tried accordingly. Mary was charged as an accessory to two counts of murder and seventy-three counts of attempted murder, for the total number of people who had been in danger from Gary's various attempts. I shuddered to know that the "three" in that "seventy-three" included myself and my son and grandson. Neither she nor Gary would see the light of day again.

I'd like to say that made me feel glad, but it did the opposite. It had all been so unnecessary. When Cliff Armstrong talked to me on the last day of shooting and thanked me once again, I gave him a long lecture about the ramifications of his behavior. He promised he would change.

I actually believed him. He had started being courteous to the cast and crew. He even said "please" when he asked for something and "thank you" when he got it. No one knew how to handle that.

I could only hope that it would continue.

I went back to my usual routine. Martin had gone back to school, so I had the weekdays to myself. I attended my book club, went out with Octavian, puttered around my garden, and caught up on my reading.

I was reading in my living room, with Dandelion curled up on my feet like a purring foot warmer, when there was a knock at the door.

After covering up the spyhole for a moment to make sure I wasn't going to get shot (I may have gotten rid of two new killers, but I still had a few old killers after me), I looked out and saw it was Liz.

I opened the door.

"Well, if it isn't my nudist detective. Come on in!"

"How's the hand?" she asked as she came in.

"Oh, it's fine. You did an excellent field dressing. Everyone was convinced you were a real nurse."

"At least I didn't need to use the defibrillator. When those fireworks went off right in front of me, I thought I was going to have a heart attack."

Within a few minutes, we were sitting in my living room, sipping tea, Dandelion curled up in my guest's lap.

"I must thank you again for all your help," I said. "You may have saved my grandson's life."

"Oh, you had the case solved without me. I just added some muscle."

"Some much-needed muscle. I drove through downtown this morning. All of the sets and trailers are gone. It feels like a ghost town. I guess Cheerville will go back to its old placid self. I'm glad, but in a way, I'll miss all those crazy film people."

Liz flashed me a mischievous grin over the rim of her teacup. "They're not all gone."

"What do you mean?"

"We had an unexpected guest at the nudist colony. One of those movie people you're missing."

"Really? Who?"

I had visions of a naked Harvey stumbling drunkenly around the colony's tennis court. It was not a pretty thought.

"You have to swear not to tell anyone."

"Who would I tell? They'd think I was a member."

"You still are a member. Your membership doesn't expire for several months."

"You know what I mean. Who is it?"

She set her teacup down, a smug smile creeping across her lips.

"Cliff Armstrong."

"No!"

"Yes. He's been a nudist for years. It's amazing he's been able to keep it out of the press. He says he spends several days at a nudist colony after every movie. It helps him unwind."

"He said he felt like he could never be himself. Perhaps that's one way he's trying. Wait, you spoke with him?"

Liz giggled. "Yes. We went swimming in the lake together."

"You went skinny-dipping. With Cliff Armstrong."

"Yes."

My teacup clattered as I set it down. My head spun. Visions of a naked Cliff Armstrong diving into that beautiful lake filled my mind's eye.

"Barbara, are you all right?"

"Oh my. I think I need that defibrillator."

ABOUT THE AUTHOR

Harper Lin is a *USA TODAY* bestselling cozy mystery author. When she's not reading or writing mysteries, she loves going to yoga classes, hiking, and hanging out with her family and friends.

For a complete list of her books by series, visit her website.

www.HarperLin.com

www.ingramcontent.com/pod-product-compliance
Lightning Source LLC
Chambersburg PA
CBHW050856180626
46814CB00007B/2759